THE DRAGON KING'S DAUGHTER

TEN TANG DYNASTY STORIES

University Press of the Pacific
Honolulu, Hawaii

The Dragon King's Daughter
Ten Tang Dynasty Stories

Translated by
Yang Hsien-Yi and Gladys Yang

ISBN 0-89875-263-9

Reprinted from the 1962 edition

University Press of the Pacific
Honolulu, Hawaii
http://www.universitypressofthepacific.com

MAP OF CHANGAN DURING THE TANG DYNASTY

LEGEND

A Jen the Fox Fairy
B Prince Huo's Daughter
C Story of a Singsong Girl
D Wu-shuang the Peerless
E The Kun Lun Slave
F The Spendthrift and the Alchemist

FOREWORD

The Tang Dynasty (618-907) was a golden age of poetry and short stories. In the brief span of two hundred and ninety years many outstanding poets and story writers appeared, including men like Li Po, Tu Fu, Pai Chu-yi, Li Kung-tso and Pai Hsing-chien, who have left works which will live for ever. Over fifty thousand poems and over four hundred stories of the Tang Dynasty are extant today, reflecting glory on China's ancient civilization and making no mean contribution to world literature.

The short story can be found in embryo form in China during the Six Dynasties (222-589), when a number of interesting anecdotes and tales appeared. But whether describing spirits or famous men, most of these stories were merely rough sketches or simple anecdotes. Hu Ying-ling (1551-1602), a Ming Dynasty critic, has written:

> During the Six Dynasties we find many weird tales, most of them not deliberately invented but based on hearsay and misconceptions. Only in the Tang Dynasty did men start writing such tales for themselves.

The Tang Dynasty, then, was the time when Chinese scholars began to write highly imaginative stories in polished language and with a wealth of detail, giving a truthful and moving picture of the people and society of the time. Poetry and the short story were the two most highly developed forms of literature of the period. As Hung Mai (1123-1202) of the Sung Dynasty wrote:

We must study the Tang stories. Even small incidents are exquisitely moving, and often — without realizing it themselves — the authors are inspired. These stories and the Tang poetry are the wonder of their age.

To understand why the short story developed so rapidly during the Tang Dynasty, we must look at the background of the time.

The Tang Dynasty was established as a result of the victory of the agrarian revolt at the end of the Sui Dynasty (581-618). Li Yuan the first Tang emperor and his son Li Shih-min took advantage of the agrarian revolt to occupy Changan and seize the fruits of the peasants' victory. At the beginning of the seventh century they completed the unification of the country and set up the Tang empire, putting an end to the four hundred years of partition, foreign invasion and chaos which had followed the fall of the Han Dynasty in 220 A.D. Li Shih-min was one of the most outstanding emperors of medieval China. He ended the threat of foreign invasion, developed China's border regions and opened up the road to the west, thereby giving fresh impetus to economic and cultural exchanges between east and west. He also carried out a series of political and economic reforms in China, restricting the building up of great estates by landlords at the expense of the peasants, lightening taxes, encouraging handicrafts, iron-smelting, silk-weaving, ship-building and commerce, and recruiting officials from successful candidates in the "civil service" examinations. These measures greatly strengthened the Tang political system, and the development of productive forces brought about a great cultural renaissance. Literature, art, music, dancing and sculpture flourished as never before. The Tang empire was not only stronger than any preceding dynasty — it was at that time the strongest, richest and most civilized country in the world.

As commerce prospered, great cities sprang up. The Tang capital Changan (now Sian), which is the setting of five of the stories in this collection, was a thriving centre of foreign trade as were Liangchou, Yangchow, Canton and other cities. Arab merchants and foreign priests and teachers came to China in large numbers — there were four to five thousand foreigners in Changan alone. The demand of the new urban class for literature and entertainment acted as an incentive to the development of poetry and all kinds of vernacular literature and minstrelsy. And this was the popular basis from which the short story developed.

Another factor to be considered in the development of Tang stories is the conflict that inevitably arose between the vigorous new urban class and all that was rotten in the old feudal order. This social conflict provided endless fresh material for short stories. Indeed, the high place accorded to the Tang stories in the history of Chinese literature is due to the fact that their authors give us a romantic yet relatively realistic and moving portrayal of the life of the times. The rivalries within the ruling class, the weaknesses of the feudal rulers, and the opposition of the people to feudal morality during the Tang Dynasty find truthful reflection in their works.

If we analyse the background of the Tang short story writers, we can understand another important factor in the development of the story. The great majority of these writers, we find, were scholars who sat for the civil service examinations. During the Six Dynasties officials had always been chosen from a few great houses, family status being the most important criterion of selection; hence the powerful clans who represented the interests of the great feudal landowners had a virtual monopoly of official appointments. In the Tang Dynasty, however, competitive examinations supervised by the central government were introduced. This meant that the sons of small landlords and merchants now had a chance to enter the ranks of the ruling class, with the result that all scholars were eager to pass the examinations.

In order to make a favourable impression on the examiner before the examination, it was customary for candidates to present him with essays or stories they had written. Chao Yen-wei in his *Sketchbook Written Below the Hill* writes:

> The Tang scholars first prevailed on some important personage to send in their names to the authorities, then presented essays to the examiner. After a few days, they would present more. These essays combined a number of literary forms, and could display the poetic gifts of the writer as well as his knowledge of history and power of logical exposition.

This explains why most of the Tang writers of short stories were scholars who had sat for the civil service examinations. These men represented a new social force and were at variance with the great feudal landowners who had hitherto held all ruling positions. And the popularity of their stories was due to the fact that they reflected the spirit and manners of their times and the thoughts and desires of the common people.

II

The ten stories in this collection can be divided into three main categories: stories of the supernatural, stories with a political theme or adventure stories, and love stories.

Supernatural events form the theme of most of the earliest stories. China had always been rich in mythology, and, after the introduction of Buddhism into the country, tales of ghosts and spirits became even more popular, so that during the Six Dynasties we find a great number of such tales. The earliest Tang story, *An Ancient*

Mirror, is made up of a number of supernatural tales about an old bronze mirror. *Jen the Fox Fairy, The Dragon King's Daughter* and *The Spendthrift and the Alchemist* all belong to this category. They differ, however, from earlier stories of the same type in having more closely knit plots and more colourful detail, being, in fact, consummate works of art imbued with all the vitality of their age.

Jen the Fox Fairy is a moving story of the love between a fox fairy and a young man named Cheng. Although Jen is a fairy, she has human characteristics. She loves Cheng dearly, and nothing can force her to be unfaithful to him. In the end she is killed by hounds, but Cheng never forgets her. It has been suggested that the hounds in this story stand for certain despots of the time.

In *The Dragon King's Daughter* we read of the love between a young scholar named Liu and the daughter of the dragon king of Tungting Lake. The dragon princess, married against her will and cruelly treated by her husband's parents, asks Liu to carry a letter to her father. When her uncle hears of her wrongs, he charges off angrily to kill her husband. Later Liu marries the dragon princess, and they both become immortal. This beautiful story served as the theme for a number of dramas written in later dynasties.

The Spendthrift and the Alchemist is an unusual story packed with suspense. The chief character is an unsuccessful young gambler who, submitted to all sorts of trials by a Taoist priest, does not falter. In the end, however, because he cannot overcome the love of a parent for his child, he loses his chance of becoming an immortal. Stories such as this show the influence of Indian Buddhist literature. They reflect both the "escapist" thought which was the outcome of a long period of war and confusion, and the conflicts of real life.

Political satires and tales of adventure are another striking type of Tang story. The *Governor of the South-*

ern Tributary State, The White Monkey, The Man with the Curly Beard and *The Kun Lun Slave* all belong to this category.

The *Governor of the Southern Tributary State* describes the life led by the highest Tang officials. Writing to show the vanity of human pomp and riches, the author exposes the outlook of the Tang officials and their preoccupation with wealth and power.

The White Monkey is the story of a monkey with supernatural powers, written as a satire on a famous scholar who looked like a monkey. By the Tang Dynasty, literature was already being used as a political weapon.

Adventure stories belong to the end of the Tang Dynasty, when the imperial power was declining. After the revolt of An Lu-shan in 755, the central government grew weaker and weaker, while local warlords (generals on the frontiers) became increasingly powerful and struggled among themselves for ascendency.

To strengthen their power and extend their territory, these warlords exploited and enslaved the common people very cruelly. And to guard against the danger of assassination, they surrounded themselves with swordsmen and trained bodyguards. The common folk, for their part, longed for heroes to appear, who would end their sufferings and overthrow the tyrants who oppressed them. Hence stories about swordsmen and popular champions were widespread. Ku Sheng in *Wu-shuang the Peerless* is the type of hero the people admired. Brave Melek, too, in *The Kun Lun Slave,* who helps his friend Tsui to meet the girl he loves, is another admirable example of this type.

Some of the best Tang stories, however, are love stories. *Prince Huo's Daughter,* the *Story of a Singsong Girl* and *Wu-shuang the Peerless* are beautiful tales which are deservedly popular. *Prince Huo's Daughter* describes the love of the poet Li Yi for Prince Huo's daughter who has become a singsong girl. The story is a tragic one, for

Li deserts his love to marry a woman from a rich family. The deserted girl falls ill with sorrow as she waits for his return; and when finally she sees Li for the last time, she reproaches him bitterly and then dies. The author evokes great sympathy for this forsaken girl.

The *Story of a Singsong Girl* is another moving tale. A young scholar Cheng squanders all he has for love of a famous singsong girl in Changan. Reduced to beggary, he suffers all manner of hardships; but later the singsong girl takes him in and persuades him to devote all his time to study, until eventually he passes the examination and becomes an official. This romantic tale was very popular in its day.

Wu-shuang the Peerless describes the trials and final marriage of Wang Hsien-ke and his cousin Wu-shuang. Wang and Wu-shuang are separated during a revolt; and when order is restored Wu-shuang's parents are put to death for having collaborated with the mutineers, while she is forced to become a palace maid. Though Wang mourns bitterly, he never gives up hope of seeing her again. And later, Ku Sheng, a champion of the oppressed, miraculously brings her back to Wang so that the two lovers can marry.

Love stories reflect most clearly the sharp conflict over marriage between the old and new classes of the Tang Dynasty. The powerful feudal clans set great store by official rank and pedigree. As rigid observers of class distinctions, they arranged their marriage alliances according to status and official rank, and their children were not allowed to marry into plebeian families. Singsong girls, it goes without saying, could not become the recognized wives of scholars; and even girls from respectable families were not free to marry as they pleased. But it is precisely the true love of characters like Prince Huo's daughter and the young scholar Cheng, untrammelled by false respect for social status or conventions, that the Tang writers praise. Faithless Li is attacked for his mercenary marriage and for deserting the girl who loves him truly. Thus we find evidence in these stories of the violent clash over marriage between the old feudal families and the new class which had grown up in the cities. The complete lack of freedom in feudal marriage is criticized, and lovers are praised who attack outworn conventions and fight for a free, happy marriage based on true love. This is why the Tang love stories, so filled with popular aspirations, were seen as ideal themes by Yuan and Ming Dynasty dramatists.

III

We have seen, then, that the Tang stories arose following the political, economic and cultural upsurge of the period. They continued the Six Dynasties tradition of supernatural tales and, influenced by contemporary art and minstrelsy and by the vernacular Buddhist literature, developed vigorously. Rich in ideological content, they reveal the various conflicts of feudal society under the centralized rule of the Tang emperors, and reflect the rich, brilliant life of the age. Of course, these stories have their limitations too. Their language is so ornate that only readers of the upper class could appreciate them. This is why, as the Tang social system broke down, such stories were superseded by the more popular vernacular literature of the Sung and Yuan Dynasties which was better adapted to the requirements of the urban class.

The stories in this collection are arranged in chronological order, together with a brief account of the author. These ten tales are a fair sample of the chief types of Tang stories, and from them we can glimpse something of China's rich and varied literary heritage.

CONTENTS

THE WHITE MONKEY
Anonymous   1

JEN THE FOX FAIRY
Shen Chi-chi   6

THE DRAGON KING'S DAUGHTER
Li Chao-wei   17

PRINCE HUO'S DAUGHTER
Chiang Fang   32

GOVERNOR OF THE SOUTHERN TRIBUTARY STATE
Li Kung-tso   44

STORY OF A SINGSONG GIRL
Pai Hsing-chien   57

WU-SHUANG THE PEERLESS
Hsueh Tiao   72

THE SPENDTHRIFT AND THE ALCHEMIST
Li Fu-yen   80

THE KUN LUN SLAVE
Pei Hsing   87

THE MAN WITH THE CURLY BEARD
Tu Kuang-ting   92

ILLUSTRATIONS

(Taken from late sixteenth or seventeenth century editions of plays based on the Tang Dynasty stories)

Facing page

"Having said this, she broke down and sobbed."   18

". . . lying there in a tipsy state, half dreaming and half awake."   44

"She . . . returned his gaze with a look of answering admiration."   58

"The carved door was not locked, and the bronze lamp inside shed a faint light."   90

". . . his appearance struck awe into them all."   96

Map of Changan during the Tang Dynasty   *Frontispiece*

THE WHITE MONKEY

Anonymous

IN the year 545, during the Liang Dynasty, the emperor sent General Lan Ching on an expedition to the south. He went as far as Kweilin, and wiped out the rebel forces of Li Shih-ku and Chen Cheh. At the same time his lieutenant Ouyang Hei fought his way as far as Changlo, conquering all the cave-dwellers there and leading his army deep into difficult terrain.

Now Ouyang's wife had a white skin and was very beautiful and delicate.

"You should not have brought such a beautiful wife here," his men told him. "There is a god in these parts who carries off young women, especially good-looking ones. You had better guard her carefully."

Ouyang took fright. That night he set guards around the house, and hid his wife in a closely guarded inner chamber with a dozen maidservants on watch. During the night a high wind sprang up and the sky turned dark, but nothing untoward happened and shortly before dawn the exhausted guards dozed off. Suddenly, however, they were startled from their sleep to find that Ouyang's wife had disappeared. The door was still locked, and no one knew how she had left. They started looking outside on the steep hillside, but a thick fog blotted out everything at one yard's distance, making it impossible to continue the search. Then dawn came, but still they could find no trace of her.

This is a satire on the famous calligrapher Ouyang Hsun who was reputed to look like a monkey.

In great anger and grief Ouyang swore that he would
not return alone. On pretext of sickness he stationed
his troops there, and sent them out daily in all directions
to search the valleys and heights for his wife. A month
later, on a bush some thirty miles away, they found one
of her embroidered shoes, soaked by rain but still rec-
ognizable. Overcome with grief, Ouyang intensified
the search, taking thirty picked armed men with rations
to scour the hills. After another ten days, they reached
a place about seventy miles from their camp from where
they could see a green, tree-clad mountain to the south
which towered above the other hills. When they came
to the foot of this mountain, they found it surrounded
by a deep stream, which they had to build a little bridge
to cross. Between the precipices and emerald bamboos
they caught glimpses of coloured dresses and heard the
sound of women talking and laughing. When they pulled
themselves up the cliffs by vines and ropes, they found
green trees planted in avenues with rare flowers between
them, and a verdant meadow fresh and soft as a carpet.
It was a quiet, secluded, unearthly retreat. There was
a gate to the east, hewn in the rock, through which
several dozen women in bright new dresses and shawls
could be seen passing — singing and laughing as they
went. When they saw the strangers, they stopped to stare.
And when the men went up to them, the women asked
what had brought them there.

After Ouyang had told them, the women looked at
each other and sighed. "Your wife has been here over
a month," they said. "Just now she is ill in bed. You
may go and see her." Passing through a wooden door
in the stone gate, Ouyang saw three spacious enclosures
where couches strewn with silk cushions had been placed
by the walls. His wife was lying on a bed spread with
matting and rugs, with rich food placed before her. At
Ouyang's approach she turned and saw him, but signed
to him to leave.

"Some of us have been here for ten years already," the other women told him, "while your wife has only just arrived. This is where the monster lives. He is a man-killer, a match for even a hundred warriors. You had better slip away before he comes back. If you will let us have forty gallons of potent wine, ten dogs for him to eat, and several dozen catties of hemp, we shall be able to kill him. Come at noon, not earlier, ten days from now." They urged him to leave quickly, and Ouyang did so.

He was back again on the appointed day bringing with him the strong liquor, hemp and dogs. "The monster is a great drinker," the women told him, "and likes to drink himself silly. When he is drunk he always wants to test his strength, and tells us to fasten his arms and legs with silken ropes as he lies on the couch. Then he frees himself with one leap. But once we twisted three ropes together he couldn't break them. Now if we twist hemp inside the silk, we are sure he will never be able to snap it. His whole body is like iron, but he invariably protects those few inches under his navel; this must be his vulnerable spot." Then, pointing to a nearby precipice, they said, "That is where he stores his food. You can conceal yourselves there. Keep quiet and wait. Put the wine by the flowers and the dogs in the forest. If our plan works we shall call you."

Ouyang and his men did as they were told, and waited with bated breath. Late in the afternoon, something like a streamer of white silk flew down from the top of a distant hill straight into the cave, and in a little while a six-foot man with a fine beard came out. Dressed in white, with a stick in his hand, he was attended by the women. He gave a start at the sight of the dogs, then leaped at them, seized them and tore them limb from limb, eating greedily until he was sated. The women offered him drinks in jade cups, and together they joked and laughed gaily. After he had drunk several pints of wine, the women helped him in, and sounds of fun and merriment could be heard.

After a long time, the women came out to summon the men, who went in carrying their weapons. They saw a huge white monkey fastened by its four paws on the couch. At the sight of the men it recoiled and struggled in vain to release itself, and its furious eyes flickered like lightning. Ouyang and his men fell on it, only to find its body like iron or stone. But when they stabbed at its belly under the navel, their swords sank in and red blood spurted out. The white monkey gave a long sigh and said to Ouyang, "This must be the will of heaven — for otherwise you would not have been able to kill me. Your wife has conceived. Don't kill the child born to her, for he will grow up to serve a great monarch and your family will prosper." With these words he died.

They searched through his possessions, and found stores of precious things as well as an abundance of rare food on the tables. Every treasure known to man was there, including several gallons of rare scents and a pair of finely wrought swords. The thirty-odd women were all exquisite beauties, some of whom had been there for ten years. They said that when women grew old they were taken away, to what fate no one knew. The white monkey was the only one to enjoy these women, for he had no followers.

Every morning the monkey would wash and put on a hat, a white collar and a white silk dress, wearing the same in winter and summer alike. He had white fur several inches long. When he stayed at home he would read wooden tablets inscribed with hieroglyphics which no one else could decipher; and after he had finished reading he would put the tablets under a stone step. On a clear day he might practise sword play, and then the two swords would encircle him like flashes of lightning making a moon-like halo round him. He ate all manner

of things, particularly nuts, and was also very partial
to dogs, whose blood he loved to drink. At noon he would
fly off to travel thousands of miles in half a day, coming
back at night. Such was his custom.

Whenever something caught his fancy, he would not
rest till it was his. At night he forwent sleep to gambol
through all the beds, enjoying the women in turn. He
could chatter away and discourse eloquently too, despite
his simian form.

One early autumn day that year when leaves were
beginning to fall, the white monkey had seemed in low
spirits and said, "I have been accused by the mountain
deities and condemned to death. But if I solicit the aid
of other spirits, perhaps I shall escape." Just after the
full moon, a fire sprang up under the stone step and
burned his tablets. "I have lived a thousand years but
never had a child," he said despondently. "Now this
woman is with child, it means my death is near." Running
his eyes over the women, he wept for a while. "This
mountain is secluded and steep, and no man has set
foot here before," he went on. "Looking down from the
peaks I have seen packs of wolves with tigers and other
wild beasts at the foot of the mountain, while not even
a woodcutter has appeared on the heights. If it were
not the will of heaven, how could men have come here?"

Ouyang then went back taking the jade, precious stones
and beautiful treasures as well as all the women, some
of whom were able to find their own homes. In a year's
time Ouyang's wife gave birth to a son, and the child
took after the monkey. Later Ouyang was condemned
to death by Emperor Wu of the Chen Dynasty. But an
old friend of his, Chiang Tsung, was partial to Ouyang's
son on account of his outstanding intelligence and took
him into his house. Thus the boy escaped death. He
grew up to become a good writer and calligrapher and a
well-known figure in his time.

JEN THE FOX FAIRY

Shen Chi-chi

WEI Yin, ninth son of the daughter of the Prince of Hsinan, was a somewhat wild young lord and a heavy drinker. His cousin's husband, Cheng, whose personal name is not known but who was the sixth child of his family, had studied the military arts and was also fond of drinking and women. Since he was poor and had no home of his own, he lived with his wife's family. Cheng and Wei became inseparable. In the sixth month of the ninth year of the Tien Pao period (750 A.D.), they were walking together through the capital on their way to a drinking party in the Hsinchang quarter, when Cheng, who had some private business, left Wei south of the Hsuanping quarter, saying he would join him later at the feast. Then Wei headed east on his white horse, while Cheng rode south on his donkey through the north gate of the Shengping quarter.

On the road Cheng came upon three girls, one of whom, dressed in a white gown, was exceedingly lovely. Pleasantly surprised, he whipped up his donkey to circle round them, but lacked the courage to accost them. Since the girl in white kept glancing at him in what seemed an encouraging way, he asked jokingly:

"Why should such beautiful girls as you travel on foot?"

The girl in white countered with a smile: "If men with mounts aren't polite enough to offer us a lift, what else can we do?"

Shen Chi-chi (c. 750-800) was a native of Soochow and a good classical scholar and historian. He is the author of "Tale of the Pillow."

"My poor donkey is not good enough for such lovely ladies as you," protested Cheng. "But it is at your disposal, and I shall be glad to follow you on foot."

He and the girl looked at each other and laughed, and with her two maids teasing them they were soon on familiar terms. He went east with these young women to Loyu Park, and dusk had fallen by the time they reached a magnificent mansion with massive walls and an imposing gate. The girl in white went in, calling back over her shoulder, "Wait a little!" One of her maids stayed at the gate and asked Cheng his name. Having told her, he enquired the name of the girl and learned that her surname was Jen and that she was the twentieth child in the family.

Presently Cheng was invited in. He had just tethered his donkey at the gate and placed his hat on the saddle, when the girl's sister — a woman of thirty or thereabouts — came out to greet him. Candles were set out, the table spread, and they had drunk several cups of wine when the girl, who had changed her dress, joined them. Then they drank a great deal and made merry, and late at night they went to bed together. Her coquetry and charm, the way she sang and laughed and moved — it was all exquisite and something out of this world. Just before dawn Jen said, "You had better go now. My brother is a member of the royal conservatory of music and serves in the royal guards. He'll be home at daybreak and he mustn't see you." Having arranged to come again, Cheng left.

When he reached the end of the street, the gate of that quarter was still bolted. But there was a foreign bread shop there where a light was burning and the stove had been lit. Sitting under the awning, waiting for the morning drum, Cheng began chatting with the shopkeeper. Pointing to where he had spent the night, he asked, "When you turn east from here you come to a big gate — whose house is that?"

"It's all in ruins," said the shopkeeper. "There's no house left."

"But I was there," insisted Cheng. "How can you say there is no house?"

The shopkeeper understood in a flash what had happened. "Ah, now I see it!" he exclaimed. "There's a fox fairy there, who often tempts men to spend the night with her. She has been seen three times. So you met her too, did you?"

Ashamed to admit the truth, Cheng denied this. When it was light he looked at the place again, and found the walls and the gate still there, but only waste land and a deserted garden behind.

After reaching home he was blamed by Wei for not joining him the previous day; but instead of telling the truth, Cheng made up an excuse. He was still bewitched by the fairy's beauty, however, and longed to see her again, unable to drive her image from his heart. About a fortnight later, in a clothes shop in the West Market, he once more came upon her accompanied by her maids. When he called out to her, she tried to slip into the crowd to avoid him; but he called her name repeatedly and pushed forward. Then, with her back to him and her fan behind her, she said: "You know who I am. Why do you follow me?"

"What if I do?" asked Cheng.

"I feel ashamed to face you," she replied.

"I love you so much, how could you leave me?" he protested.

"I don't want to leave you; I'm only afraid you must hate me."

When Cheng swore that he still loved her and became more insistent in his request, the girl turned round and let fall the fan, appearing as dazzlingly beautiful as ever.

"There are many fox fairies about," she told the young man. "It's just that you don't know them for what they are. You needn't think it strange."

Cheng begged her to come back to him and she said, "Fox fairies have a bad name because they often harm men; but that is not my way. If I have not lost your favour, I would like to serve you all my life." Asked where they could live, she suggested, "East of here you'll come to a house with a big tree towering above its roof. It's in a quiet part of town — why not rent it? The other day when I first met you south of the Hsuanping quarter, another gentleman rode off on a white horse towards the east. Wasn't he your brother-in-law? There's a lot of furniture in his house you can borrow."

It so happened, indeed, that Wei's uncles, absent on official duty, had stored away their furniture with him. Acting on Jen's advice, Cheng went to Wei and asked to borrow it. Asked the reason, he said, "I have just got a beautiful mistress and rented a house for her. I want to borrow the furniture for her use."

"A beauty, indeed!" retorted Wei with a laugh. "Judging by your own looks, you must have found some monstrosity!"

None the less his friend lent him curtains, bed and bedding, dispatching an intelligent servant with him to have a look at the girl. Presently the servant ran back, out of breath and sweating. "Well?" asked Wei, stepping forward. "Have you seen her? What's she like?"

"Marvellous! I've never seen anyone so lovely!"

Wei, who had many relations and had seen many beauties in the course of his numerous adventures, asked whether Cheng's mistress was a match for one of these.

"No comparison!" exclaimed the servant. Wei mentioned four or five other names, but still received a negative reply. His sister-in-law, sixth daughter of the Prince of Wu, was a peerless beauty, as lovely as a fairy.

"How does she compare with the sixth daughter of the Prince of Wu?" he asked.

But again his man declared that there was no comparison.

"Is that possible?" Wei exclaimed, clasping his hands in amazement. Then he hastily asked for water to wash his neck, put on a new cap, rouged his lips and went to call on Cheng.

It happened that Cheng was out and Wei, entering, found a young servant sweeping and a maid at the door, but no one else. He questioned the boy, who told him with a laugh that there was no one at home. But making a search of the rooms, Wei saw a red skirt behind a door and going closer discovered Jen hiding there. Dragged out from the dark corner, she was even more beautiful than he had been told. Mad with passion, he took her in his arms to assault her, only to meet with resistance. He pressed her hard, until she said, "You shall have your way, but first let me recover my breath." However, when Wei came on again she resisted as before. This happened three or four times. Finally Wei held her down with all his strength and the girl, exhausted and drenched with perspiration, knew she could hardly escape. Limp and inert, she gave him a heart-rending look.

"Why are you so sad?" he asked.

With a long sigh, she answered, "I pity Cheng with all my heart."

"What do you mean?" he demanded.

"He's over six feet tall but has failed to protect a woman — how can he call himself a man? You are young and rich, and have many beautiful mistresses. You have seen many like me. But Cheng is a poor man, and I am the only woman he loves. How can you rob him of his only love while you have so many? Because he is poor, he has to be dependent on others. He wears your clothes, eats your food, and so he is in your power.

If he could support himself, we shouldn't have come to this."

At this, Wei, a gallant man with a sense of justice, desisted, composed himself and apologized. Then Cheng came back and they exchanged cordial greetings. And thenceforward Wei looked after all their needs.

Jen often met Wei and went out with him on foot or by carriage. He spent almost every day with her until they became the best of friends, taking great delight in each other's company. And because she was everything to him except his mistress, he loved and respected her and grudged her nothing. Even eating and drinking he could not forget her. Knowing Wei's love for her, Jen said to him one day: "I'm ashamed to accept such favours from you. I don't deserve such kindness. And I can't betray Cheng to do as you desire. I was born in Shensi and brought up in the capital. My family are theatre people, and since all the women in it are the mistresses and concubines of rich men, they know every single courtesan in the capital. If you see some beautiful girl and cannot have her, I would like to get her for you to repay your kindness." Wei accepted her offer.

A dress-maker named Chang in the market place took Wei's fancy with her clear complexion and fine figure. He asked Jen if she knew her, and she answered, "She is my cousin. I can get her easily." After about ten days, she brought this woman to him. A few months later, when Wei was tired of Chang, Jen said, "Market girls are easy game. Try to think of someone most charming but hardly attainable, and I shall do my best for you."

"The other day at the Han Shih Festival,"[1] said Wei, "I went to Chienfu Temple with some friends when General Tiao had brought his musicians to play in the

---

[1] On this day in early spring no stoves were lit and people ate cold food (*han shih*).

hall. One of them was a reed-organ player, a girl of about sixteen with two locks of hair over her ears. She was charming — quite lovely! Do you know her?"

"She's the general's favourite," answered Jen. "Her mother is my sister. I'll see what I can do."

Wei bowed to her, and Jen promised him her help. She became a frequent visitor at the general's house. After a whole month had passed, Wei urged her to make haste and enquired what her plan was. She asked him for two bolts of silk to use as a bribe, and these he gave to her. Two days later, he was having a meal with Jen when the general sent his steward with a black horse to beg her to go to his house. Hearing this summons, Jen smiled at Wei and said, "It is done!" It seemed that she had made the favourite fall ill with a disease which medicine was powerless to cure. At their wits' end, the girl's mother and the general had consulted a witch doctor; but Jen had shown this witch doctor her house and bribed her to say that the sick girl must be removed there.

Accordingly the witch doctor told the general, "The girl must not stay at home but should go and live in that house in the southeast, to imbibe the life-giving influences there." When they made enquiries and found it was Jen's house, the general asked her to let the girl lodge there. At first Jen declined, saying her house was too small, and only after repeated requests did she give her consent. Then the general sent the girl in a carriage with clothing and trinkets, accompanied by her mother, to Jen's house. As soon as she arrived, she was cured. Within a few days, Jen secretly introduced Wei to her, and a month later she was with child. But then her mother took fright, and carried her back hastily to the general; so this was the end of that affair.

One day Jen asked Cheng, "Can you lay your hands on five or six thousand coins? If so, I promise to make a profit for you."

When he had raised a loan of six thousand coins, she told him, "Go to the horse-dealers in the market. You will find a horse with a spot on its rump — buy it and take it home."

Cheng went to the market where he saw a man trying to sell a horse which, sure enough, had a black mark on its rump. Accordingly he bought it and led it home. His brothers-in-law scoffed, "Nobody wants a hack like that. What did you buy such a crock for?"

Soon after that, Jen told him: "The time has come to sell the horse. You should get thirty thousand for it." Then Cheng took the horse to the market, and was offered twenty thousand but refused to sell.

All the folk in the market marvelled: "Why does one offer such a price? Why does the other refuse to sell?"

When Cheng started to ride away, the would-be purchaser followed him to the gate and raised his offer to twenty-five thousand, but still Cheng would not sell. "Nothing doing under thirty thousand," he declared. Then, however, his brothers-in-law gathered round and pestered him into selling at just under thirty thousand.

Later he found out the reason for the buyer's insistence: This man was the groom of Chaoyin County, and one of his horses which had a black mark on its rump had died three years before. This fellow was to be discharged soon, and was due to be paid sixty thousand for keeping the horses. If he could buy a horse for half that sum and hand it over to the government, he would still be the gainer. He would be paid for three years' fodder which had never been consumed. That was why he had insisted on buying.

Once Jen asked Wei for some new dresses, as her old gowns were worn out. He wanted to buy silk for her, but she declined, saying she preferred ready-made clothes. Wei commissioned a shopkeeper named Chang to get them, sending him to Jen to find out just what she wanted. When the shopkeeper saw her, he was so as-

tonished that later he said to Wei, "That is no common
woman, she must be from some noble house. It isn't
right for you to keep her. I hope you will return her to
her family soon, to avoid trouble." This shows how
striking her appearance was.

However, they could not understand why she insisted
on buying ready-made dresses instead of having them
made to measure.

A year later Cheng was appointed a captain of Huaili
Prefecture, with his headquarters at Chincheng. Now
since Cheng had a wife, though he spent the day with his
mistress he had to go home to sleep at night, and he
missed Jen. So when he was going to his post he asked
her to accompany him; but she refused.

"We should only be together for a month or two," she
said. "It seems hardly worth it. It would be better to
work out how much I shall need to spend while you're
away, and let me wait at home till you come back."
Although Cheng pleaded with her, she was adamant.
Then Cheng asked Wei for a loan, and Wei came to persuade her too and to ask the reason. After some little
hesitation she answered, "A witch told me it would be
unlucky for me to go west this year. That's why I want
to stay here."

But Cheng was so eager for her to go, he could think
of nothing else. Both men laughed at her and demanded,
"How can an intelligent girl like you be so superstitious?"
They reasoned with her.

"If what the witch said was true," said Jen, "and I die
because I go with you, won't you be sorry?"

"Nonsense!" declared the two men, and insisted again.
Finally they persuaded her against her will.

Wei lent her his horse and saw them off at Linkao. The
next day they reached Mawei. Jen was riding ahead
on the horse with Cheng behind on his donkey, followed
by her maid and other attendants. The gamekeepers
outside the West Gate had been training their hounds at

Lochuan for some ten days, and just as Jen was passing the hounds leaped out from the bushes. Then Cheng saw his mistress drop to the ground, turn into a fox and fly southwards with the pack in hot pursuit. He ran forward and yelled at the hounds, but could not restrain them; and after running a few hundred yards she was caught. Shedding tears, Cheng took money from his pocket to buy back the carcass, which was then buried with a pointed stick stuck into the ground to mark the place. When he looked back, her horse was cropping grass by the roadside, her clothes were lying on the saddle, while her shoes and stockings were hanging on the stirrups like the skin shed by a cicada. Her trinkets had dropped to the ground, but everything else belonging to her had vanished, including her maid.

About ten days later Cheng returned to the capital. Wei was delighted to see him, and coming forward to greet him asked, "Is Jen well?"

With tears Cheng replied, "She is dead!"

Wei was stricken with grief at this news. They embraced each other and mourned bitterly, then Wei asked what sudden illness had carried her off.

"She was killed by hounds," answered Cheng.

"Even fierce hounds cannot kill men," protested Wei.

"But she was no human being."

When Wei cried out in amazement, his friend told him the whole story. He could only marvel and heave sigh after sigh. The next day they went together by carriage to Mawei, and after opening the grave to look at the carcass returned prostrated with grief. When they thought back over her behaviour, the only unusual habit they could recall was that she would never have her clothes made to measure.

Later Cheng became the inspector of the royal stable and a very wealthy man, keeping a stable of some dozen horses. He died at the age of sixty-five.

During the Ta Li period (766-779), I was staying at Chungling and spent much time with Wei, who told me this story over and over again until I knew it inside out. Later Wei became a chancellor of the imperial court and concurrently Prefect of Lungchou, finally dying at his post in the northwest.

It is sad to think that a beast assuming human form should resist violation and remain chaste and faithful to her lord till death, while few women nowadays are equal to this! And what a pity that Cheng was not more intelligent. He simply appreciated her appearance without studying her nature. A really wise man would have probed the laws of change, investigated the nature of supernatural beings, and with his skilful pen recorded the gist of the mystery, instead of simply contenting himself with the enjoyment of her grace and charm. This is most unfortunate!

In the second year of the Chien Chung period (781), when I was Left Advisor, I left for Soochow at the same time that General Pei Chi, Junior City Magistrate Sun Cheng, Minister Tsui Hsu of the Civil Affairs Ministry, and Right Advisor Lu Shun were setting out to the Yangtse Valley. We travelled together from the province of Shensi to Soochow by land and along the waterways. With us too was ex-Advisor Chu Fang, who was on a tour. As we floated down the Ying and Huai Rivers in our boat, feasting by day and conversing at night, each of us told of some strange happenings. When these gentlemen heard the story of Jen, they were deeply moved and greatly astonished; and because they asked me to record this strange tale, I have written this narrative.

THE DRAGON KING'S DAUGHTER

Li Chao-wei

DURING the Yi Feng period (676-678), a scholar named Liu Yi failed in the official examination and, as he was returning to the Hsiang River Valley, decided to go and take his leave of a fellow provincial who was staying at Chingyang. He had ridden about two miles, when a bird flying up from the ground startled his horse and made it bolt and it had galloped two miles before he could stop it. Then he caught sight of a girl herding sheep by the roadside. She was amazingly beautiful but her finely arched eyebrows were knit, her clothes were soiled, and she was standing there listening intently as if awaiting someone's arrival.

"What has brought you to such a wretched state?" Liu asked.

The girl first expressed her gratitude with a smile; then, unable to restrain her tears, replied, "Unhappy creature that I am! Since you ask me the reason, how can I hide the deep resentment I feel? Listen then! I am the youngest daughter of the dragon king of Tungting Lake. My parents married me to the second son of the dragon king of the Ching River; but my husband, devoted to pleasure and led astray by his attendants, treated me more unkindly every day. I complained to his parents, but they were too fond of their son to take my part. When I persisted in complaining, they grew angry and banished me here." Having said this, she broke down and sobbed.

Li Chao-wei (c. 800) was a native of Lunghsi (present-day Kansu Province).

"Tungting Lake is so far away," she went on. "It lies beyond the distant horizon, and I can get no word to my family. My heart is breaking and my eyes are worn out with watching, but there is no one to know my grief or pity me. Since you are going south and will pass near the lake, may I trouble you to take a letter?"

"I have a sense of justice," answered Liu, "and your story makes my blood boil. I only wish I had wings to fly there — why talk of trouble? But the lake is very deep, and I can only walk on land. How am I to convey your message? I fear I may be unable to get through, proving unworthy of your trust and failing in my own sincere wish to help you. Can you tell me how to make the journey?"

"I cannot say how I appreciate your kindness," said the girl, shedding tears. "If ever I receive a reply, I shall repay you even if it costs my life. Before you promised to help me, I dared not tell you how to reach my parents; but actually, to go to the lake is no harder than going to the capital."

Asked for directions, she told him, "South of the lake stands a big orange tree which is the sacred tree of the village. Take off this belt, put on another, and knock on the trunk three times. Someone will come to your call, and if you follow him you will have no difficulty. I have opened my heart to you besides trusting you with my letter. Please tell my parents what you have heard. On no account fail me!"

Liu promised to do as she said. Then the girl took a letter from her pocket and handed it to him with a bow, all the while looking eastwards and weeping in a way that touched his heart.

When he had put the letter in his wallet, he enquired, "May I ask why you herd sheep? Do deities also eat cattle?"

"No," she answered. "These are not sheep, but rain-bringers."

Having said this, she broke down and sobbed

"What are they?"

"Thunder, lightning, and the like."

Liu looked at the sheep closely, and saw that they moved proudly with heads held high. They cropped the grass differently too, although they were the same size as ordinary sheep and had the same wool and horns.

"Now that I am going to act as your messenger," he said, "I hope in future, when you get back to the lake, you won't refuse to see me."

"Certainly not!" she exclaimed. "I shall treat you as a dear relative."

Then they bid each other goodbye, and he started east. After a few dozen yards he looked back, but both girl and sheep had disappeared.

That evening he reached the county town and said goodbye to his friend. It took him over a month to get home, and he went without delay to Tungting Lake. He found the orange tree south of the lake, changed his belt, faced the tree and knocked three times. A warrior came out of the water, and bowed to him. "Why have you come here, honourable sir?" he asked.

Without telling him the story, Liu simply answered, "To see your king."

The warrior parted the waves and pointed the way, saying to Liu as he led him down, "Close your eyes. We will be there in no time."

Liu did as he was told, and soon they reached a great palace where he saw clustered towers and pavilions, millions of gates and arches, and all the rare plants and trees of the world. The warrior asked him to wait at the corner of a great hall.

"What place is this?" asked Liu.

"The Palace of the Divine Void."

Looking round, Liu saw that this palace was filled with every precious object known to man. The pillars were of white jade, the steps of jasper; the couches were of coral, the screens of crystal. The emerald lintels were set with cut glass, while the rainbow-coloured beams were inlaid with amber. And the whole created an impression of strange beauty and unfathomable depth which defied description.

The dragon king was a long time in coming, and Liu asked the warrior, "Where is the Lord of Tungting?"

"His Majesty is in the Dark Pearl Pavilion," was the reply. "He is discussing the Fire Canon with the Sun Priest, but will have finished soon."

"What is the Fire Canon?" Liu wanted to know.

"Our king is a dragon," was the reply, "so water is his element, and with one drop of water he can flood mountains and valleys. The priest is a man, so fire is his element, and with one torch he can burn down a whole palace. Since the properties of the elements differ, they have different effects. As the Sun Priest is expert in the laws of men, our king has asked him over for a talk."

He had barely finished speaking when the palace gate opened, a mist seemed to gather and there appeared a man in purple holding a jasper sceptre. The warrior leaped to attention, crying, "This is our king!" Then he went forward to report Liu's arrival.

The dragon king looked at Liu and asked, "Are you not of the world of men?"

Liu replied that he was, and bowed. The king greeted him in return and asked him to be seated.

"Our watery kingdom is dark and deep, and I am ignorant," said the dragon king. "What has brought you, sir, from such a distance?"

"I am of the same district as Your Majesty," replied Liu. "I was born in the south, but have studied in the northwest. Not long ago, after failing in the examination, I was riding by the Ching River when I came upon your daughter herding sheep in the open country. Exposed to wind and rain, she was a pitiful sight. When questioned, she told me she had come to such a pass because of her husband's unkindness and his parents' neglect. I assure you, her tears as she spoke went to my heart. Then she entrusted this letter to me and I promised to deliver it. That is why I am here." He took out the letter and passed it to the king.

After reading the missive, the king covered up his face and wept. "Though I am her old father," he lamented, "I have been like a man blind and deaf, unaware that my child was suffering far away, while you, a stranger, came to her rescue. As long as I live, I shall never forget your kindness." He gave way to weeping, and all the attendants shed tears.

Presently a palace eunuch approached the king, who handed him the letter with orders to tell the women in the inner palace. Soon wailing was heard from within and in alarm the king bade his attendants, "Quickly tell the women not to make so much noise, or the Prince of Chientang may hear them!"

"Who is this prince?" asked Liu.

"My younger brother," said the dragon king. "He used to be the Prince of the Chientang River, but has now retired."

"Why must you keep it from him?"

"Because he is overbold," was the reply. "The nine years of flood in the time of the ancient sage King Yao was due to one of his rages. Not long ago he quarrelled with the angels in heaven and flooded the five mountains. Thanks to a few good deeds I had to my credit, the heavenly emperor pardoned him; but he has to be kept here. The people of Chientang are waiting still for his return."

He had scarcely finished when there came a great crash, as if both heaven and earth had been torn asunder. The palace shook and mist seethed as in burst a crimson dragon more than a thousand feet long, dragging after it a jade pillar to which its neck had been fastened by a gold chain. Its eyes were bright as lightning, its tongue red as blood, and it had scarlet scales and a fiery mane.

Thunder crashed and lightning flashed around it, then snow and hail fell thick and fast, after which it soared up into the azure sky.

Panic-stricken, Liu had fallen to the ground. But now the king himself helped him up, urging, "Have no fear! All is well."

After a long time, Liu recovered a little. And when calm enough he asked leave to withdraw. "I had better go while I can," he explained. "I couldn't survive another experience like that."

"There's no need to leave," said the king. "That's the way my brother goes, but he won't come back that way. Do stay a little longer." He called for wine, and they drank to pledge their friendship.

Then a soft breeze sprang up, wafting over auspicious clouds. Amid flying pennons and flags and the sound of flutes and pipes, in came thousands of brightly dressed, laughing and chattering girls. Among them was one with beautiful, arched eyebrows who was wearing bright jewels and a gown of the finest gauze. When she drew near, Liu saw that she was the girl who had given him the message. Now she was shedding tears of joy, as she moved through a fragrant red and purple mist to the inner palace.

The king said with a laugh to Liu, "Here comes the prisoner from the Ching River!" He excused himself and went inside, and from the inner palace happy weeping was heard. Then the king came out again to feast with Liu.

Presently a man in purple strode up to stand by the king. He was holding a jasper sceptre and looked vigorous and full of spirit. The king introduced him as the Prince of Chientang.

Liu stood up to bow, and the prince bowed in return. "My unhappy niece was insulted by that young blackguard," he said. "It was good of you, sir, with your strong sense of justice, to carry the news of her wrongs so far.

If not for you, she would have pined away by the Ching River. No words can express our gratitude."

Liu bowed and thanked him. Then the prince told his brother, "I reached the river in one hour, fought there for another hour, and took another hour to come back. On my return journey I flew to high heaven to report to the heavenly emperor; and when he knew the injustice done he pardoned me. In fact, he pardoned my past faults as well. But I am thoroughly ashamed that in my indignation I did not stop to say goodbye, upsetting the whole palace and alarming our honourable guest." He bowed again.

"How many did you kill?" asked the king.

"Six hundred thousand."

"Did you destroy any fields?"

"About three hundred miles."

"Where is that scoundrel, her husband?"

"I ate him."

The king looked pained.

"Of course that young blackguard was insufferable," he said. "Still, that was going rather far. It is lucky that the heavenly emperor is omniscient and pardoned you because such a great injustice had been done. Otherwise what could I have said in your defence? Don't ever do that again!" The prince bowed once more.

That evening Liu was lodged in the Hall of Frozen Light, and the next day another feast was given at the Emerald Palace. All the royal family gathered there, music was played, and wine and delicacies were served. Then bugles, horns and drums sounded as ten thousand warriors danced with flags, swords and halberds on the right-hand side, while one came forward to announce that this was the triumphal march of the Prince of Chientang. This spectacular and awe-inspiring display impressed all who saw it.

Then to an accompaniment of gongs and cymbals, stringed and bamboo instruments, a thousand girls dressed in bright silks and decked with jewels danced on the left-hand side, while one came forward to announce that this music was to celebrate the return of the princess. The melodies were poignant and sweet, breathing such grief and longing that all who heard were moved to tears. When the two dances were over, the dragon king in high good humour made the dancers presents of silk. Then the guests sat down together to feast, and drank to their hearts' content.

When they had drunk their fill, the king rapped on table and sang:

> *Wide the earth and grey the sky,*
> *Who can hear a distant cry?*
> *The fox lies snugly in his lair,*
> *But thunderbolts can reach him there.*
> *A true man, who upholds the right,*
> *Restored my daughter to my sight.*
> *Such service how can we requite?*

After the king's song ended, the prince made a bow and sang:

> *Life and death are fixed by fate,*
> *Our princess found a worthless mate.*
> *By River Ching she had to go,*
> *In wind and frost, in rain and snow.*
> *This gentleman her letter bore,*
> *Then we restored her to this shore.*
> *This we'll remember evermore!*

After this song, the king and prince stood up and each presented a cup to Liu, who hesitated bashfully before accepting, then quaffed off the wine, returned the cups and sang:

> *Like a blossom in the rain,*
> *The princess longed for home in vain,*
> *I brought back tidings of her plight,*
> *And all her wrongs were soon set right,*

Now we feast, but soon must part,
For home again I needs must start.
Bitter longing fills my heart!

This song of his was greeted by loud applause.

The king brought out a jasper casket of rhinoceros horn which could part the waves, and the prince an amber dish bearing jade that shone at night. They presented these to Liu, who accepted the gifts with thanks. Then the inmates of the palace started piling silk and jewels beside him, until gorgeous materials were heaped up all around. Laughing and chatting with the company, he had not a moment's quiet. Sated at last with wine and pleasure, he excused himself and went back to sleep in the Hall of Frozen Light.

The next day he was feasting again in the Pavilion of Limpid Light when the Prince of Chientang, heated with wine and lounging on the couch, said insolently, "A hard rock can be smashed but not made to yield, and a gallant man can be killed but not put to shame. I have a proposal to make. If you agree, all will be well between us. If not, we can perish together. How about it?"

"Let me hear your proposal," said Liu.

"As you know, the wife of the Lord of the Ching River is our sovereign's daughter," said the prince. "She is an excellent girl with a fine character, well thought of by all her kinsmen but unlucky enough to have suffered indignities at the hands of that scoundrel. However, that's a thing of the past. We would like to entrust her to you, and become your relatives for ever. Then she who owes you gratitude will belong to you, and we who love her will know she is in good hands. A generous man shouldn't do things by halves. Don't you agree?"

For a moment Liu looked grave. Then he rejoined with a laugh, "I never thought the Prince of Chientang would have such unworthy ideas. I have heard that once when you crossed the nine continents, you shook the five mountains to give vent to your anger; and I have seen you break the golden chain and drag the jade pillar after you to rescue your niece. I thought there was no one as brave and just as you, who dared risk death to right a wrong, and would sacrifice your life for those you love. These are the true marks of greatness. Yet now, while music is being played and host and guest are in harmony, you try to force me to do your will in defiance of honour. I would never have expected this of you! If I met you on the angry sea or among dark mountains, with your fins and beard flying and mist and rain all around, though you threatened me with death I should consider you a mere beast and not count it against you. But now you are in human garb. You talk of manners and show a profound understanding of human relationships and the ways of men. You have a nicer sense of propriety than many gallants in the world of men, not to say monsters of the deep. Yet you try to use your strength and temper — while pretending to be drunk — to force me to agree to your proposal. This is hardly right. Although small enough to hide under one of your scales, I am not afraid of your anger. I hope you will reconsider your proposal."

Then the prince apologized. "Brought up in the palace, I was never taught etiquette," he said. "Just now I spoke wildly and offended you — your rebuke was well deserved. Don't let this spoil our friendship." That night they feasted together again as merrily as ever, and Liu and the prince became great friends.

The day after, Liu asked permission to leave. The queen gave another feast for him in the Hall of Hidden Light, which was attended by a great throng of men and women, maids and servants. Shedding tears, the queen said to him, "My daughter owes you so much, we can never repay you. And we are sorry to have to say good-bye." She told the princess to thank him.

"Shall we ever meet again?" asked the queen.

Liu regretted now that he had not agreed to the prince's request. His heart was very heavy. After the feast, when he bid them farewell, the whole palace was filled with sighing, and countless rare jewels were given him as parting gifts.

He left the lake by the way he had come, escorted by a dozen or more attendants who carried his bags to his home before leaving him. He went to a jeweller's at Yangchow to sell some of the jewels, and though he parted with about one hundredth only he became a multi-millionaire, wealthier by far than all the rich men west of the Huai River.

He married a girl called Chang, but soon she died. Then he married a girl called Han; but after several months she died as well, and Liu moved to Nanking.

Loneliness tempted him to marry again, and a go-between told him, "There is a girl called Lu from Fanyang County, whose father, Lu Hao, used to be magistrate of Chingliu. In his later years he studied Taoist philosophy and lived by himself in the wilderness, so that now no one knows where he is. Her mother was named Cheng. The year before last the girl married into the Chang family at Chingho, but unfortunately her husband died. Because she is young, intelligent and beautiful, her mother wants to find a good husband for her. Are you interested?"

So Liu married this girl on an auspicious day, and since both families were wealthy, the magnificence of their gifts and equipage impressed the whole city of Nanking.

Coming home one evening about a month after their marriage, Liu was struck by his wife's resemblance to the dragon king's daughter, except that she was in better health and more lovely. Accordingly, he told her what had happened.

"I can't believe it," she replied. Then she told him that she was with child, and Liu became more devoted to her than ever.

A month after the child was born, Liu's wife dressed herself in fine clothes, put on her jewels, and invited all their relatives to the house. Before the assembled company she asked him with a smile, "Don't you remember meeting me before?"

"Once I carried a message for the dragon king's daughter," he replied. "That is something I have never forgotten."

"I am the dragon king's daughter," she said. "Wronged by my former husband, I was rescued by you, and I swore to repay your kindness. But when my uncle the prince suggested that we marry, you refused. After our separation we lived in two different spheres, and I had no way of sending word to you. Later my parents wanted to marry me to another river god — that stripling of the Chochin River — but I remained true to you. Although you had forsaken me and there was no hope of seeing you again, I would rather have died than stop loving you. Soon after that, my parents took pity on me and decided to approach you again; but you married girls from the Chang and Han families, and there was nothing we could do. After those girls had died and you came to live here, my family felt the match was possible. But I never dared hope that one day I might be your wife. I shall be grateful and happy all my life, and die without regret." So saying, she wept.

Presently she went on: "I did not disclose myself to you before, because I knew you did not care for my looks. But I can tell you now that I know you are attached to me. I am not good enough to keep your love, so I'm counting on your fondness for the child to hold you. Before I knew you loved me, I was so anxious and worried! When you took my letter, you smiled at me and said, 'When you go back to the lake, don't refuse to see me!' Did you want us to become husband and wife in future? Later when my uncle proposed the marriage and you refused him, did you really mean it or were you just offended? Do tell me!"

"It must have been fated," said Liu. "When first I met you by the river, you looked so wronged and pale, my heart bled for you. But I think all I wanted at the time was to pass on your message and right your wrong. When I said I hoped you wouldn't refuse to see me in future, that was just a casual remark with nothing behind it. The prince's attempt to force me into marriage annoyed me because I object to being bullied. Since a sense of justice had motivated my action, I could hardly marry the woman whose husband's death I had caused. As a man of honour I had to do what I thought right. So during our drinking I spoke from my heart, saying only what was just, with no fear of him. Once the time came to leave, however, and I saw the regret in your eyes, I was rather sorry. But after I left the lake, the affairs of this world kept me too occupied to convey my love and gratitude to you. Well, now that you belong to the Lu family and are a woman, I find my former feelings towards you were more than a fleeting passion after all! From now on, I shall love you always."

His wife was deeply moved and replied with tears, "Don't think human beings alone know gratitude. I shall repay your kindness. A dragon lives for ten thousand years, and I shall share my span of life with you. We shall travel freely by land and sea. You can trust me."

"I never thought you could tempt me with immortality!" laughed Liu.

They went to the lake again, where the royal entertainment once more given them beggars description.

Later they lived at Nanhai for forty years. Their mansions, equipage, feasts and clothes were as splendid as those of a prince, and Liu was able to help all his relatives. His perennial youth amazed everybody. During the Kai Yuan period (713-741), when the emperor set his heart on discovering the secret of long life and searched far and wide for alchemists, Liu was given no peace and went back with his wife to the lake. Thus he disappeared from the world for more than ten years. At the end of that period, his younger cousin, Hsueh Ku, lost his post as magistrate of the capital and was sent to the southeast. On his journey Hsueh crossed Tungting Lake. It was a clear day and he was looking into the distance when he saw a green mountain emerging from the distant waves. The boatmen shrank back in fear, crying, "There was never any mountain here — it must be a sea monster!"

As they were watching the mountain approach, a painted barge came swiftly towards them and the men on it called Hsueh's name. One of them told him, "Master Liu sends his greetings." Then Hsueh understood. Invited to the foot of the mountain, he picked up the skirt of his gown and went quickly ashore. On the mountain were palaces like those on earth, and Liu was standing there with musicians before and bejewelled girls behind him, more splendid than in the world of men. Talking more brilliantly and looking even younger than formerly, he greeted Hsueh at the steps and took his hand.

"We have not been separated long," he said, "yet your hair is turning grey."

"You are fated to become an immortal and I to become dry bones," retorted Hsueh with a laugh.

Liu gave him fifty capsules, and said, "Each of these will give you an extra year of life. When you have finished them, come again. Don't stay too long in the world of men, where you must undergo so many hardships." They feasted happily, and then Hsueh left. Liu was never seen again, but Hsueh often related this story. And fifty years later, he too vanished from the world.

This tale shows that the principal species of each category[1] of living creatures possesses supernatural powers — for how otherwise could reptiles assume the virtues of men? The dragon king of Tungting showed himself truly magnanimous, while the Prince of Chientang was impetuous and straightforward. Surely their virtues did not appear from nowhere. Liu's cousin, Hsueh Ku, was the only other human being to penetrate to that watery kingdom, and it is a pity that none of his writings have been preserved. But since this account holds such interest, I have recorded it here.

---

[1] The ancient Chinese divided the animal kingdom into five categories: feathered, furred, hard-shelled, scaly and hairless. The chief species of these categories were phoenix, unicorn, tortoise, dragon and man. From man, the most intelligent of all, these others derived some of their virtues.

PRINCE HUO'S DAUGHTER

Chiang Fang

DURING the Ta Li period (766-779), there was a
young man of Lunghsi whose name was Li Yi. At the
age of twenty he passed one of the civil service examinations and the following year the best scholars of his rank
were to be chosen for official posts through a further
examination at the Ministry of Civil Affairs. In the
sixth month he arrived at the capital and took lodgings
in the Hsinchang quarter. He came from a good family,
showed brilliant promise, and was acknowledged by his
contemporaries as unsurpassed in literary craftsmanship.
Thus even senior scholars looked up to him. Having no
mean opinion of his own gifts, he hoped for a beautiful
and accomplished wife. But long and vainly did he search
among the famous courtesans of the capital.

In Changan there was a match-maker named Pao, who
was the eleventh child in her family. She had been a
maidservant in the prince consort's family, but a dozen
years before this had redeemed herself and married.
Clever and with a ready tongue, she knew all the great
families and was a past master at arranging matches. Li
gave her rich gifts and asked her to find him a wife, and
she was very well disposed towards him.

One afternoon, some months later, Li was sitting in
the south pavilion of his lodgings when he heard insistent
knocking and Pao was announced. Gathering up the

Chiang Fang lived at the beginning of the ninth century. He
has left a volume of poetry as well as this story which won
him fame.

skirt of his gown, he hurried to meet her. "What brings you here so unexpectedly, madam?" he asked.

Pao laughed and responded, "Have you been having sweet dreams? A fairy has come down to earth who cares nothing for wealth but who admires wit and gallantry. She is made for you!"

When Li heard this he leaped for joy and felt as if he were walking on air. Taking Pao's hand he bowed and thanked her, saying: "I shall be your slave as long as I live!"

Asked where the girl lived and what her name was, Pao replied: "She is the youngest daughter of Prince Huo. Her name is Jade, and the prince doted on her. Her mother, Chingchih, was his favourite slave. When the prince died, his sons refused to keep the child because her mother was of humble birth, so they gave her a portion and made her leave. She has changed her name to Cheng, and people do not know that the prince was her father. But she is the most beautiful creature you ever saw, with a sensibility and grace beyond compare. She is well versed too in music and the classics. Yesterday she asked me to find a good match for her, and when I mentioned your name she was delighted, for she knows you by reputation. They live in Old Temple Lane in the Shengyeh quarter, in the house at the entrance to the carriage drive. I have already made an appointment for you. Go tomorrow at noon to the end of the lane, and look for a maid called Kueitse. She will show you the house."

As soon as the match-maker left, Li started to prepare for the great occasion, sending his servant Chiuhung to borrow a black charger with a gilt bit from his cousin Shang who was adjutant general of the capital. That evening he washed his clothes, had a bath, and shaved. He could not sleep all night for joy. At dawn he put on his cap and examined himself in the mirror, fearing all

might not go well. Having frittered away the time till
noon, he called for the horse and galloped to the Shengyeh
quarter. When he reached the place appointed, he saw
a maid standing there waiting for him, who asked, "Are
you Master Li?" He dismounted, told the maid to stable
the horse, and went quickly in, bolting the gate behind
him.

The match-maker came out from the house, smiling at
him from a distance as she cried, "Who is this gate-
crasher?" While they were joking with each other, he
found himself led through the inner gate into a courtyard
where there were four cherry trees and a parrot cage
hanging on the northwest side.

At the sight of Li, the parrot squawked, "Here's a
guest! Lower the curtain!"

Naturally bashful, Li had felt some scruples about
going in, and now the parrot startled him and brought
him to a standstill until Pao led the girl's mother down
the steps to welcome him, and he was asked to go inside
and take a seat opposite her. The mother, little more
than forty, was a slender, attractive woman with charming manners.

"We have heard of your brilliance as a scholar," she
said to Li, "and now that I see what a handsome young
man you are too, I am sure your fame is well deserved.
I have a daughter who, though lacking in education, is
not ill-favoured. She should be a suitable match for you.
Madame Pao has already proposed this, and today I would
like to offer my daughter to you in marriage."

"I am a clumsy fellow," he replied, "and do not deserve
such a distinction. If you accept me, I shall count it a
great honour as long as I live."

Then a feast was laid, Jade was called by her mother
from the east chamber, and Li bowed to greet her. At
her entrance, he felt as if the room had been transformed
into a bower of roses, and when their eyes met he was

dazzled by her glance. The girl sat down beside her
mother, who said to her, "You like to repeat those lines:

'When the wind in the bamboos rustles the curtain,
I fancy my old friend is near.'

Here is the author of the poem. You have been reading
his works so often — what do you think of him now you
see him?"

Jade lowered her head and answered with a smile: "He
doesn't live up to my expectations. Shouldn't a poet be
more handsome?"

Then Li got up and made several bows. "You love
talent and I admire beauty," he said. "Between us we
have both!"

Jade and her mother looked at each other and smiled.

When they had drunk several cups of wine together,
Li stood up and asked the girl to sing. At first she declined, but her mother insisted, and in a clear voice she
sang an intricate melody. By the time they had drunk
their fill it was evening, and the match-maker led the
young man to the west wing to rest. The rooms were
secluded in a quiet courtyard, and the hangings were
magnificent. Pao told the maids Kueitse and Wansha
to take off Li's boots and belt. Then Jade herself appeared. With sweet archness and charming coyness she
put off her clothes. Then they lowered the bed-curtains,
lay down on the pillows and enjoyed each other to their
hearts' content. The young man felt that he was in bed
with a goddess.

During the night, however, the girl suddenly gazed at
him through tears and said, "As a courtesan, I know I am
no match for you. You love me now for my looks, but I
fear that when I lose them your feelings will change, and
then I shall be like a vine with nothing to cling to, or a
fan discarded in the autumn. So at the height of my
joy I cannot help grieving."

Li was touched, and putting his arm round her neck said gently, "Today I have attained the dream of my life. I swear I would sooner die than leave you. Why do you talk like that? Let me have some white silk to pledge you my faith in writing."

Drying her tears, Jade called her maid Yingtao to raise the curtain and hold the candle, while she gave Li a brush and ink. When not occupied with music, Jade was fond of reading, and her writing-case, brushes and ink all came from the palace. Now she brought out an embroidered case and from it took three feet of white silk lined with black for him to write on. The young man had a gift for contemporary composition, and taking up the brush wrote rapidly. He swore by the mountains and rivers, by the sun and the moon, that he would be true. He wrote passionately and movingly, and when he had finished he gave Jade his pledge to keep in her jewel box.

After that they lived happily for two years like a pair of kingfishers soaring on high, together day and night. But in the spring of the third year, Li came first in his examination and was appointed secretary-general of Cheng County. In the fourth month, before leaving to take up his post and to visit his parents in Loyang, he gave a farewell party to all his relatives at the capital. It was the season between spring and summer. When the feast was over and the guests had gone, the young man and the girl were filled with grief at their coming separation.

"With your talents and fame," said Jade, "you have many admirers who would like to be related to you by marriage. And your old parents at home have no daughter-in-law to look after them. So when you go to take up this post, you are bound to find a good wife. The pledge you made me is not binding. But I have a small request to make, which I hope you will consider. May I tell you what it is?"

Li was startled and protested, "In what way have I offended you, that you speak like this? Tell me what is in your mind, and I promise to do whatever you ask."

"I am eighteen," said the girl, "and you are only twenty-two. There are still eight years before you reach thirty, the age at which a man should marry. I would like to crowd into these eight years all the love and happiness of my life. After that you can choose some girl of good family for wife — it will not be too late. Then I shall retire from the world, cutting my hair short and becoming a nun. This is the wish of my life and I ask no more."

Cut to the heart, Li could not hold back his tears. "I swear by the bright sun," he assured the girl, "as long as I live I shall be true to you. My only fear is that I may fail to please you — how can I think of anything else? I beg you not to doubt me, but rest assured. I shall reach Huachou in the eighth month and send to fetch you. We shall be together again before very long." A few days later he said goodbye to her and went east.

Ten days after Li's arrival at his post, he asked leave to go to Loyang to see his parents. Before he reached home, his mother had arranged a match for him with a cousin in the Lu family — a verbal agreement had already been reached. His mother was so strict that Li, though hesitating, dared not decline; accordingly he went through with the ceremonies and arranged a date for the wedding. Since the girl's family was a powerful one, they demanded over a million cash betrothal money and would call off the marriage if this were not forthcoming. Because Li's family was poor he had to borrow this sum; and he took advantage of his leave to look up distant friends, travelling up and down the Huai and Yangtse River valleys from the autumn till the next summer. Knowing that he had broken his promise to fetch Jade at the appointed time, he sent no message to her, hoping that she would give him up. He also asked his friends not to disclose the truth.

When Li failed to return at the appointed time, Jade tried to find out what had become of him, only to receive contradictory reports. She also consulted many fortune-tellers and oracles. This went on for more than a year, until at last she fell ill of sorrow; and, lying in her lonely room, went from bad to worse. Though no tidings had come from Li, her love for him did not falter, and she gave presents to friends and acquaintances to persuade them to find news of him. This she did so persistently that soon all her money had gone and she often had to send her maid out secretly to sell dresses and trinkets through an inn-keeper in the West Market.

One day Jade sent Wansha to sell an amethyst hair-pin, and on her way to the inn the maid met an old jade-smith who worked in the palace. When he saw what she was carrying, he recognized it. "This hair-pin is one I made," he said. "Many years ago, when Prince Huo's youngest daughter first put up her hair, he ordered me to make this pin and gave me ten thousand cash for the job. I have always remembered it. Who are you? And how did you come by this?"

"My mistress is the prince's daughter," replied the maid. "She has come down in the world, and the man she married went to Loyang and deserted her. So she fell ill of grief, and has been in a decline for two years. Now she wants me to sell this, so that she can bribe someone to get news of her husband."

The jade-smith shed tears, exclaiming, "Can the children of nobles fall on such evil times? My days are nearly spent, but this ill-fated lady's story wrings my heart."

Then the old man led Wansha to the house of Princess Yenhsien, and when the princess heard this story she too heaved sigh after sigh. Finally she gave the maid one hundred and twenty thousand cash for the hair-pin.

Now the girl to whom Li was engaged was in the capital. After raising the sum he needed for his marriage, he returned to his post in Cheng County; but at the end of the year he again asked for leave to go to Changan to get married. And he found quiet lodgings, so that his whereabouts would not be known. A young scholar, however, named Tsui Yun-ming, who was Li's cousin and a kind-hearted man, had formerly drunk with Li in Jade's room and laughed and talked with her until they were on the best of terms. Whenever he received news of Li, he would tell Jade truthfully, and she had helped him so often with money and clothing that he felt deeply indebted to her.

When Li came to the capital, Tsui told Jade, who sighed and exclaimed indignantly, "How can he be so faithless?" She begged all her friends to ask Li to come to her; but knowing that he had broken his promise and that the girl was dying, he felt too ashamed to see her. He took to going out early and coming back late in order to avoid callers. Though Jade wept day and night, unable to eat or sleep in her longing to see him, he never came. And indignation and grief made her illness worse. When the story became known in the capital, all the young scholars were moved by the girl's love while all the young gallants resented Li's heartlessness.

It was then spring, the season for pleasure trips, and Li went one day with five or six friends to Tsungching Temple to see the peonies in bloom. Strolling in the west corridor, they composed poems together. A close friend of Li's named Wei Hsia-ching, a native of Changan, was one of the party. "Spring is beautiful and flowers are in bloom," he told Li. "But your old love nurses her grief in her lonely room. It is really cruel of you to abandon her. A true man would not do this. Think it over again!"

As Wei was sighing and reproaching Li, up came a
young gallant wearing a yellow silk shirt and carrying a
crossbow.

He was handsome and splendidly dressed, but attended
only by a Central Asian boy with cropped hair. Walking
behind them, he overheard their conversation; and
presently he stepped forward and bowed to Li, saying,
"Is your name not Li? My family comes from the east,
and we are related to the royal house. Though I have
no literary talent myself, I value it in others. I have
long been an admirer of yours and hoped to make your
acquaintance, and today I am lucky enough to meet you.
My humble house is not far from here, and I have musicians to entertain you. I have eight or nine beautiful
girls too, and a dozen good horses, all of them at your disposal. I only hope you will honour me with a visit."

When Li's friends heard this, they were delighted.
They rode along after this young gallant, who swiftly
turned corner after corner until they reached the
Shengyeh quarter. Since they were approaching Jade's
house, Li was reluctant to go any farther and made some
excuse to turn back.

But the stranger said: "My humble home is only a
stone's throw from here. Don't leave us now!" He took
hold of Li's bridle and pulled his horse along.

In a moment they had reached the girl's house. Li
was dismayed and tried to turn back, but the other
quickly ordered attendants to help him dismount and
lead him inside. They pushed him through the gate and
bolted it, calling out, "Master Li is here!" Then excla-
mations of joy and surprise could be heard from the
whole house.

The night before, Jade had dreamed that Li was brought
to her bedside by a man in a yellow shirt and that she
was told to take off her shoes. When she woke up she
told her mother this dream, and said, "Shoes symbolize
union. That means that husband and wife will meet

again. But to take them off means separation. We shall be united then parted again — for ever. Judging by this dream, I shall see him once more and after that I shall die."

In the morning she asked her mother to dress her hair for her. Her mother thought she was raving and paid no attention, but when Jade insisted she consented. And no sooner was her hair done than Li arrived.

Jade had been ill so long that she could not even turn in bed without help. But on hearing that her lover had come she got up swiftly, changed her clothes and hurried out like one possessed. Confronting Li in silence, she fixed angry eyes on him. So frail she could hardly stand, she kept averting her face and then, against her will, looking back, till all present were moved to tears.

Soon several dozen dishes of food and wine were brought in. And when the company asked in astonishment where this feast had come from, they found it had been ordered by the young gallant. The table spread, they sat down. Jade, though she had turned away from Li, kept stealing long glances at him; and finally raising her cup of wine, she poured a libation on the ground and said, "I am the unhappiest of women, and you are the most heartless of men. Dying young of a broken heart, I shall not be able to look after my mother; and I must bid farewell for ever to my silk dresses and music, to suffer torments in hell. This is your doing, sir! Farewell! After death I shall become an avenging spirit and give your wives and concubines no peace."

Grasping Li's arm with her left hand, she threw her cup to the ground. Then, after crying out several times, she fell dead. Her mother placed her body on Li's knee and told him to call her, but he could not revive her.

Li put on mourning and wept bitterly during the wake. The night before the obsequies she appeared to him within the funeral curtain, as beautiful as in life. She was wearing a pomegranate-red skirt, purple tunic, and red

and green cape. Leaning against the curtain and finger-
ing the embroidered tassels, she looked at him and said,
"You must still have some feeling for me, to see me off.
That is a comfort to me here among the shades." With
that she vanished. The next day she was buried at Yusu-
yuan near the capital. After mourning by her grave, Li
went back; and a month later he married his cousin. But
he was in low spirits after all that had happened.

In the fifth month, Li went with his wife to his post at
Cheng County. About ten days after their arrival, he
was sleeping with his wife when he heard soft hoots
outside the curtain, and looking out he saw a very handsome young man hiding behind the hangings and
beckoning repeatedly to his wife. Li leaped up in agita-
tion and went round the curtain several times to look for
the intruder, but no one was there. This made him so
suspicious that he gave his wife no peace until some
friends persuaded him to make it up and he began to feel
a little better. About ten days later, however, he came
home to find his wife playing her lute on the couch, when
an engraved rhinoceros-horn case, little over an inch in
diameter and tied with a flimsy silk love-knot, was
thrown into the room. This case fell on his wife's lap.
When Li opened it, he found two love-peas, one Spanish
fly as well as other aphrodisiacs and love-charms. Howl-
ing like a wild beast in his anger, he seized the lute and
beat his wife with it as he demanded the truth. But she
could not clear herself. After that he often beat her
savagely and treated her with great cruelty; and finally he
denounced her in the court and divorced her.

After Li divorced his wife, he soon became suspicious
of the maidservants and women slaves whom he had
favoured, and some he even killed in his jealousy. Once
he went to Yangchow and bought a famous courtesan
named Ying, who was the eleventh child of her family.
She was so charming and beautiful that Li was very fond
of her. But when they were together he liked to tell her

about another girl he had purchased, and how he had
punished her for various faults. He told her such things
every day to make her fear him, so that she would not
dare to take other lovers. Whenever he went out, he
would leave her on the bed covered up with a bath-tub
which was sealed all round; and upon his return he would
examine the tub carefully before letting her out. He also
kept a very sharp dagger and would say to his maids,
"This is Kehsi steel. It's good for cutting the throats of
unfaithful women!"

Whatever women he had, he would soon grow suspicious of them, and he was a jealous husband to the two
other wives he married later.

GOVERNOR OF THE SOUTHERN
TRIBUTARY STATE

Li Kung-tso

C HUNYU Fen, a native of Tungping and a well-known
gallant of the Yangtse River region, was fond of
drinking, hot-tempered and recklessly indifferent to conventions. He had amassed great wealth and acted as patron
to many dashing young men. Because of his military
prowess he had been made an adjutant of the Huainan
Army, but in a fit of drunkenness he offended his general
and was dismissed. Then in his disappointment he let
himself go and gave his days to drinking.

Chunyu's home was some three miles east of Yangchow.
South of his house there was a huge old ash tree with
great branches, thick with foliage, which shaded an acre
of land; and under this tree Chunyu and his boon companions drank daily to their hearts' content. In the ninth
month of the tenth year of the Chen Yuan period (794),
Chunyu got drunk, and two of his friends carried him
home and laid him in the eastern chamber. "You had
better have a sleep," they said, "while we give the horses
some fodder and wash our feet. We shan't go until you
feel better."

He took off his cap and rested his head on the pillow,
lying there in a tipsy state, half dreaming and half
awake. Presently he saw two messengers in purple, who
entered to kneel before him and announce, "His Majesty

Li Kung-tso (c. 770-850) was a friend of the writer Pai Hsing-
chien. Three other stories by him are extant.

. . . lying there in a tipsy state, half dreaming and half awake

the king of Ashendon has sent us, his humble subjects,
to invite you to his kingdom."

Chunyu arose from his couch, dressed himself and
followed the messengers to the gate, where he found a
small green carriage drawn by four horses. Seven or
eight attendants standing there helped him into this.
Driving out of the gate, they made for the ash tree and—
to Chunyu's amazement — headed down the hollow under
the tree. However, he dared ask no questions. The scenery
along the road — the mountains and rivers, trees and
plants — looked different from the world of men. The
climate too had changed. After they had travelled about
ten miles, city walls came into sight, and the highway
began to be thronged with carriages and people. The
footmen on the carriage kept calling out to clear the road
and the pedestrians moved hurriedly out of their way.
They entered a great city through a turreted red gate over
which was inscribed in letters of gold "The Great Kingdom of Ashendon." The gate-keepers bestirred themselves and bowed low to them.

Then a rider cantered up, calling, "As His Highness
the prince consort has travelled so far, His Majesty orders
him to be taken to the East Hostel to rest." And he led
the way.

Chunyu saw a gate in front swing open, and alighting
from the carriage he passed through it. Here were brightly
painted and finely carved balustrades and pilasters among
terraces of blossoming trees and rare fruits, while tables
and rugs, cushions and screens had been set ready in the
hall where a rich feast was laid out. Chunyu was en-
chanted. Presently it was announced that the prime
minister had arrived, and Chunyu went to the foot of
the hall steps to await him respectfully. Dressed in purple
and holding an ivory sceptre, the minister approached,
and they paid their respects to each other. This done,
the minister said, "Though our land is far from yours,

our king has invited you here because he hopes for an alliance with you by marriage."

"How can a humble person like myself aspire so high?" replied the young man.

The minister asked Chunyu to follow him to the palace. They walked a hundred yards and entered a red gate where spears, axes, and halberds were displayed and among several hundred officers who stood by the side of the road to make way for them was Chunyu's old drinking friend Chou. Chunyu was secretly delighted, but dared not go forward to accost him.

Then the minister led Chunyu up to a court where guards were standing solemnly in formation, showing that they were in the royal presence. He saw a tall, imposing figure on the throne, wearing a white silk robe and a bright red cap. Overcome by awe, he did not look up, but bowed as he was directed by the attendants. "At your father's wish," said the king, "we have asked you to our unworthy kingdom to offer you our second daughter as your wife." When Chunyu kept his head lowered and dared not reply, the king told him, "You may go back to the guest house and prepare for the ceremony."

As the minister accompanied him back, Chunyu was thinking hard. Since his father was a frontier general who had been reported missing, it was possible that, having made peace with the border kingdoms, he was responsible for this invitation. Still the young man was bewildered and at a loss to account for it.

That evening, amid pomp and splendour, betrothal gifts of lambs, swans and silk were displayed. There was music of stringed and bamboo instruments, feasting by the light of lanterns and candles, and a concourse of carriages and horsemen. Some of the girls present were addressed as the nymphs of Huayang or Chinghsi, others as the fairies of the upper or lower region. Attended by a large retinue, they wore green phoenix head-dresses, gold cloud-like garments and golden trinkets and precious stones that dazzled the eye. These girls frolicked and played charming tricks on Chunyu who found it hard to answer their clever repartee.

"On the last Spring Purification Festival,"[1] one girl said, "I went with Lady Lingchih to Chanchih Monastery to watch Yuyen perform the Brahmana dance in the Indian Quadrangle. I was sitting with the girls on the stone bench on the north side when you and your young gallants arrived, and got off your horses to watch. You accosted us and teased us and made jokes — don't you remember how Chiungying and I tied a scarlet scarf on the bamboo? Then, on the sixteenth of the seventh month, I went with Shang Chen-tse to Hsiaokan Monastery to listen to Monk Chihsuan discoursing on the Avalokiteshvara sutra. I donated two gold phoenix-shaped hair-pins and my friend one rhinoceros-horn case. You were there too, and asked the monk to let you see them. After admiring them and praising the workmanship at some length, you turned to us and said, 'These pretty things and their owners surely can't belong to the world of men!' Then you asked my name and wanted to know where I lived, but I wouldn't tell you. You kept staring at me as if you were quite lovelorn — don't you remember?"

Chunyu replied by quoting the song:

> Deep in my heart it is hidden,
> How can I ever forget?

And the girls said, "Who could imagine that you would become our relative?"

Just then up came three men in magnificent clothes. Bowing to Chunyu, they declared, "By His Majesty's order we have come to be your groomsmen." One of them looked like an old friend.

---

[1] On this festival, which falls on the third day of the third month, people used to bathe in the rivers to "purify" themselves and so guard against evil during the coming year.

"Aren't you Tien Tse-hua of Fengyi?" Chunyu asked him. When the other said that he was, Chunyu stepped forward to grasp his hand and they talked about the past.

Asked how he came to be there, Tien replied, "On my travels I met Lord Tuan, the prime minister, and he became my patron." When Chunyu enquired if he knew of Chou's presence there, he answered, "Chou has done very well. He is now the city commandant and has great influence. On several occasions he has done me a favour."

They talked cheerfully until it was announced that the prince consort should go to the wedding. As the three groomsmen handed him his sword, pendants, robes and head-dress and helped him put them on, Tien said, "I never thought to attend such a grand ceremony for you today. You mustn't forget your old friends."

Several dozen fairy maids now began to play rare music, piercingly tender and infinitely sad, the like of which Chunyu had never heard before. Dozens of other attendants held candles all the way down a mile-long path lined on both sides with gold and emerald-green screens vividly painted and intricately carved. He sat up straight in the carriage, rather nervous, while Tien joked to put him at his ease. The girls he had seen were arriving too in phoenix-winged carriages. When he reached the gate of Hsiu Yi Palace, the girls were there too, and Chunyu was asked to alight. He went through a ceremony just like that in the world of men, at the end of which screens and fans were removed, enabling him to see his bride, the Princess of the Golden Bough. She was about fifteen, lovely as a goddess and well trained in the marriage ceremony.

After the wedding Chunyu and the princess came to love each other dearly, and his power and prestige increased daily. His equipage and entertainments were second only to the king's. One day the king took him and some other officials as his guards to hunt on the

Divine Tortoise Mountain in the west, where there were high peaks, wide marshlands and luxuriant forests stocked with all kinds of birds and beasts. The hunters came back with a big bag of game that evening.

Another day Chunyu said to the king, "On my wedding day Your Majesty told me you had sent for me in compliance with my father's wishes. My father served formerly as a general at the frontier. After a defeat he was reported missing, and I have had no news of him for eighteen years. Since Your Majesty knows where he is now, I would like to call on him."

"Your father is still serving at the northern frontier," replied the king quickly. "We are in constant touch. You had better just write to him. There is no need for you to go there." The king ordered the princess to prepare gifts to send to her father-in-law, and after a few days a reply came in his handwriting. He expressed his longing for his son and wrote just as in former letters, asking whether certain relatives were still alive and what news there was of their home-town. Since the distance between them was so great, he said, it was difficult to send news. His letter was sad and full of grief. He told Chunyu not to come, but promised that they would meet in three years' time. With this letter in his hands, Chunyu wept bitterly, unable to restrain himself.

One day the princess asked him, "Don't you ever want to take up an official post?"

"I am used to a carefree life," he answered. "I don't understand official work."

"Just take a post," she said, "and I will help you." Then she spoke to the king.

A few days later the king said, "All is not well in my southern tributary state, and the governor has been dismissed. I would like to use your talents to set their affairs in order. You might go there with my daughter." When Chunyu consented, the king ordered those in charge to get his baggage ready. Gold, jade and silk, cases and servants, carriages and horsemen formed a long baggage train when he and the princess were ready to leave. And since Chunyu had mixed with gallants as a young man and never dreamed of becoming an official, he found this most gratifying.

He sent a memorandum to the king, saying, "As the son of a military family, I have never studied the art of government. Now that I have been given this important post, I fear I shall not only disgrace myself but ruin the prestige of the court. I would therefore like to seek far and wide for wise and talented men to help me. I have noticed that City Commandant Chou of Yingchuan is a loyal, honest officer, who firmly upholds the law and would make a good minister. Then there is Tien Tse-hua, a gentleman of Fengyi, who is prudent and full of stratagems and has probed deeply into the principles of government. I have known both these men for ten years. I understand their talents and consider them trustworthy, and therefore I ask to have Chou appointed the chief councillor and Tien the minister of finance of my state. For then the government will be well administered and the laws well kept." The two men were then appointed to these posts by the king.

The evening of Chunyu's departure, the king and queen gave a farewell feast for him south of the capital.

"The southern state is a great province," said the king. "The land is rich and the people prosperous, and you must adopt a benevolent policy there. With Chou and Tien assisting you, I hope you will do well and come up to our expectations."

Meantime the queen told the princess, "Your husband is impetuous and fond of drinking, and he is still young. A wife should be gentle and obedient. I trust you to look after him well. Though you will not be too far from us, you will no longer be able to greet us every morning and evening, and I find it hard not to shed tears now that you are going away." Then Chunyu and the princess bowed, got into their carriage and started south. They talked cheerfully on the way, and several days later reached their destination.

The officials of the province, the monks and priests, elders, musicians, attendants and guards had all come out in welcome. The streets were thronged, while drums and bells could be heard for miles around. Chunyu saw a goodly array of turrets and pavilions as he entered the great city gate, above which was inscribed in letters of gold "The Southern Tributary State." In front there were red windows and a large gate with a fine view into the distance. After his arrival he studied the local conditions and helped all who were sick or distressed, entrusting his government to Chou and Tien, who administered the province well. He remained governor there for twenty years, and the people benefiting from his good rule sang his praises and set up tablets extolling his virtue or built temples to him. As a result, the king honoured him even more: he was given fiefs and titles and exalted to the position of a grand councillor of state, while both Chou and Tien also became well-known as good officials, and were promoted several times. Chunyu had five sons and two daughters. His sons were given official posts reserved for the nobility, while his daughters were married into the royal family. Thus his fame and renown were unrivalled.

One year the kingdom of Sandalvine attacked this province, and the king ordered Chunyu to raise an army to defend it. Chunyu made Chou commander of thirty thousand troops to resist the invaders at Jade Tower City, but Chou proved proud and reckless, underestimating the enemy. His troops were routed and, abandoning his armour, he fled back alone to the provincial capital at night. Meanwhile the invaders, after capturing their baggage train and arms, had withdrawn. Chunyu had Chou arrested and asked to be punished, but the king pardoned them both.

That same month Chou developed a boil on his back
and died. Ten days later the princess died of illness too,
and Chunyu's request to leave the province and accompany the hearse to the capital was granted.   Tien, the
minister of finance, was appointed deputy in his place.
Bowed down with grief, Chunyu followed the hearse. On
the way many people wept, officers and common citizens
paid their last homage, while great crowds blocked the
way and clung to the carriage. When he reached Ashendon, the king and queen were waiting outside the capital,
wearing mourning and weeping. The princess was post-
humously entitled Shun Yi (Obedient and Graceful).
Guards, canopies and musicians were provided, and she
was buried at Coiling Dragon Mount some three miles
east of the city. During the same month, Chou's son
Yung-hsin also arrived with his father's hearse.

Now though Chunyu had been ruling over a tributary
state outside the kingdom for many years, he had managed to keep on good terms with all the nobles and in-
fluential officers at court. After his return to the capital
he behaved unconventionally and gathered around himself many associates and followers, his power growing so
rapidly that the king began to suspect him. Then some
citizens reported to the king that a mysterious portent
had appeared and the state was doomed to suffer a great
catastrophe: the capital would be removed and the ancestral temples destroyed. This would be caused by some
man of foreign birth who was close to the royal family.
After deliberation the ministers decided that there was
danger in Chunyu's luxury and presumption; accordingly
the king deprived him of his attendants and forbade him
to have any further dealings with his associates, ordering
him to live in retirement.

Conscious that he had not governed badly all these
years in his province, but was being slandered, Chunyu
was in low spirits. The king, sensing this, said to him,
"You have been my son-in-law for more than twenty

years. Unhappily my daughter died young and could not live with you till old age. This is a great misfortune." Then the queen took charge of his children herself, and the king said, "You have left your home for a long time. You had better go back now for a while to see your relatives. Leave your children here and do not worry about them. In three years we shall fetch you back."

"Isn't this my home?" asked Chunyu. "What other home have I to go back to?"

"You came from the world of men," replied the king with a laugh. "This is not your home." At first Chunyu felt as if he were dreaming, but then he remembered how he had come there and, shedding tears, asked for permission to return. The king ordered his attendants to see him off, and with a bow Chunyu took his leave.

The same two messengers dressed in purple accompanied him out of the gate. But there he was shocked to see a shabby carriage with no attendants or envoys to accompany him. He got into the carriage, however, and after driving some miles they left the city behind. They travelled the same way that he had first come by. The mountains, rivers and plains were unchanged, but the two messengers with Chunyu looked so seedy that he felt let down. When he asked them when they would reach Yangchow, they went on singing without paying any attention. Only when he insisted did they answer, "Soon."

Presently they emerged from the hollow and Chunyu saw his own village unchanged. Sadness seized him, and he could not help shedding tears. The two messengers helped him down from the carriage, through the door of his house and up the steps. Then he saw himself lying in the eastern chamber, and was so frightened that he dared not approach. At that the two messengers called his name aloud several times, and he woke up.

He saw his servants sweeping the courtyard. His two guests were still washing their feet by the couch, the

slanting sun had not yet set behind the west wall and
his unfinished wine was still by the east window — but
he had lived through a whole generation in his dream!
Deeply moved, he could not help sighing. And when he
called his two friends and told them, they were equally
amazed. They went out to look for the hollow under the
ash tree, and Chunyu, pointing to it, said, "This is where
I went in the dream."

His friends believed this must be the work of some fox
fairy or tree spirit, so servants were ordered to fetch an
axe and cut through the tree trunk and branches to find
where the hollow ended. It was some ten feet long, ter-
minating in a cavity lit by the sun and large enough to
hold a couch. In this were mounds of earth which resem-
bled city walls, pavilions and courts, and swarms of ants
were gathered there. In the ant-hill was a small, reddish
tower occupied by two huge ants, three inches long, with
white wings and red heads. They were surrounded by a
few dozen big ants, and other ants dared not approach
them. These huge ants were the king and queen, and this
was the capital of Ashendon.

Then the men followed up another hole which lay
under the southern branch of the tree and was at least
forty feet long. In this tunnel there was another ant-hill
with small towers, which swarmed with ants. This was
the southern tributary state which Chunyu had governed.
Another large, rambling tunnel of a fantastic shape ran
westwards for twenty feet, and in this they found a rotten
tortoise shell as big as a peck measure, soaked by rain
and covered by luxuriant grass. This was the Divine
Tortoise Mountain, where Chunyu had hunted. They
followed up yet another tunnel more than ten feet long
in the east, where the gnarled roots of the tree had
twisted into the shape of a dragon. Here there was a
small earthen mound about a foot high, and this was the
grave of the princess, Chunyu's wife.

As he thought back, Chunyu was very shaken, for all that they had discovered coincided with his dream. He would not let his friends destroy these ant-hills, and ordered that the tunnels be covered up as before. That night, however, there was a sudden storm, and the next morning when he examined the holes the ants had gone. Thus the prophecy that Ashendon would suffer a great catastrophe and that the capital would be removed was realized. Then he thought of the invasion by the kingdom of Sandalvine, and asked his two friends to trace it. They found that some six hundred yards east of his house was a river-bed long since dry, and next to it grew a big sandal tree so thickly covered with vines that the sun could not shine through it. A small hole beside it, where a swarm of ants had gathered, must be the kingdom of Sandalvine.

If even the mysteries of ants are so unfathomable, what then of the changes caused by big beasts in the hills and woods?

At that time Chunyu's friends Chou and Tien were both in Liuho County, and he had not seen them for ten days. He sent a servant posthaste to make enquiries, and found that Chou had died of a sudden illness, while Tien was lying ill in bed. Then Chunyu realized how empty his dream had been, and that all was vanity too in the world of men. He therefore became a Taoist and abstained from wine and women. Three years later he died at home, in his forty-seventh year, just as predicted in the dream.

In the eighth month of the eleventh year of the Chen Yuan period (795), while on a journey from Soochow to Loyang I had stopped at Huaipu and met Chunyu by chance. I questioned him and looked at the ant-hills, going into his story very thoroughly. Believing it to be quite genuine, I have written this tale for those who may be interested. Although it deals with supernatural and unorthodox things, it may have a moral for the ambitious. Let future readers not think this narrative a mere series of coincidences, and let them beware of taking pride in worldly fame and position!

For, as Li Chao, former adjutant general of Huachow commented:

> *His reputation reaches to the skies,*
> *His influence can make a kingdom fall,*
> *And yet this pomp and power, after all,*
> *Are but an ant-heap in the wise man's eyes.*

STORY OF A SINGSONG GIRL

Pai Hsing-chien

IN the Tien Pao period (742-756) the Lord of Yingyang, whose name and surname I will omit, was Governor of Changchou. He was highly respected and extremely rich. When our story starts he was fifty and had a son of nearly twenty — an intelligent lad of outstanding literary ability, the admiration of all his contemporaries. His father loved him dearly and had high hopes of him. "This," he would say, "is the 'thousand-league colt' of our family." When the time came for the lad to take the provincial examination, his father gave him fine clothes and equipage for the journey, and money for his expenses in the capital. "With your gifts you should succeed at the first attempt," he said. "But I am giving you an allowance for two years, and a generous one at that, to enable you to work without worrying." The young man was quite confident too, and saw himself passing the examination as clearly as he saw the palm of his own hand.

Setting out from Changchou he reached the capital in little more than a month and took a house in the Pucheng quarter. One day on his way back from the East Market, he entered the eastern gate of the Pingkang quarter to visit a friend who lived in the southwest part. When he reached Mingko Lane, he saw a house with a rather narrow gate and courtyard. The house itself, however, was a grand one, and from the gate you could see many

---

Pai Hsing-chien (776-826) was the brother of the famous poet Pai Chu-yi. His other works include the story "The Three Dreams."

buildings stretching back. One half of the double door
was open and at it stood a girl, attended by her young
maid. She was of an exquisite, bewitching beauty, such
as the world had seldom seen.

When he saw her, the young man unconsciously reined
in his horse and hesitated, unable to tear himself away.
He deliberately dropped his whip and waited for his
servant to pick it up, all the time staring at the girl. She,
for her part, returned his gaze with a look of answering
admiration. But in the end he went away without daring
to speak to her.

After that he was like a man distracted, and secretly
begged a friend who knew the capital well to find out
who she was.

"The house belongs to a courtesan named Li," his
friend told him.

"Is it possible to get her?" he asked.

"She is very well off," said his friend, "because her
previous dealings have been with rich and aristocratic
families, who paid her lavishly. Unless you spend a million cash, she will have nothing to do with you."

"All I want is to win her," answered the young man.
"I don't mind if she costs a million."

Some days later he put on his best clothes and set out,
with a train of attendants behind him, for her house.
When he knocked at the door, a young maid opened it.

"Can you tell me whose house this is?" the young man
asked.

The maid did not answer, but ran back into the house
calling out at the top of her voice: "Here's the gentleman
who dropped his whip the other day!"

The girl replied with evident pleasure: "Ask him in.
I'll come as soon as I've changed my clothes and tidied
myself."

The young man hearing this was inwardly overjoyed
as he followed the maid into the house. He saw the
girl's mother — a grey-haired woman with a bent back —

*She . . . returned his gaze with a look of
answering admiration*

and bowing low said to her: "I hear that you have a vacant courtyard which you might be willing to let. Is that true?"

"I am afraid it is too shabby and small for a gentleman like you," she said. "You may take it if you like, but I wouldn't dare ask for any rent." She then took him into the reception room, which was a very splendid one, and asked him to be seated, saying: "I have a daughter who is very young and has few accomplishments, but who enjoys the company of visitors. I should like you to meet her."

With that she called for her daughter. The girl had sparkling eyes and dazzling white arms, and moved with such consummate grace that the young man could only leap to his feet in confusion and did not dare raise his eyes. When they had greeted each other, he made a few remarks about the weather, conscious as he did so that her beauty was such as he had never seen before.

They sat down again. Tea was made and wine poured out. The vessels used were spotlessly clean. He stayed on until it was late and the curfew drum could be heard all around, when the old lady asked if he lived far away.

He answered untruthfully: "Several miles beyond Yenping Gate," hoping that they would ask him to stay.

"The drum has sounded," she said. "You will have to leave at once, if you don't want to break the law."

"I was enjoying myself so much," said the young man, "that I didn't notice how late it was. My house is a long way off, and I have no relations in the city. What am I to do?"

"If you don't think our house too shabby," put in the girl, "what harm would there be in your spending the night here?"

He glanced several times at the old lady, who assented.

Calling his servants, he ordered them to bring two bolts of silk[1] which he offered for the expenses of a feast. But the girl stopped him and protested laughingly: "No, you are our guest. We would like to entertain you tonight with our humble household's rough and ready fare. You can treat us another time." He tried to refuse, but in the end she had her way, and they all moved to the western hall. The curtains, screens, blinds and couches were of dazzling splendour, the toilet-boxes, coverlets and pillows the height of luxury. Candles were lighted and an excellent meal was served.

After supper, when the old lady had retired, the young man and girl began to talk intimately, laughing and joking completely at their ease.

"I passed your house the other day," said the young man, "and you happened to be standing at the door. After that, I couldn't get you out of my head. Lying down to rest or sitting down to eat, I couldn't stop thinking of you."

"It was just the same with me," she answered.

"You know, I didn't come today simply to look for lodgings," he said. "I came hoping you would grant the wish of my life. But I wasn't sure what my fate would be. . . ."

As he was speaking the old woman came back and asked what they were saying. Upon being told, she laughed and said: " 'There is a natural attraction between the sexes.' When lovers are agreed, not even their parents can control them. But my daughter is of humble birth — are you sure she is fit to share your bed?"

The young man immediately came down from the dais and, bowing low, said: "Please accept me as your servant!" After that the old lady regarded him as her son-in-law; they drank heavily together and finally parted.

---

[1] In the Tang Dynasty silk was often used as money.

Next morning he had all his baggage brought round to their house and made it his home.

Henceforward he shut himself up there, and his friends heard no more of him. He mixed only with actors, dancers and people of that kind, passing the time in wild sports and aimless feasting. When his money was spent he sold his horses and men-servants. In little over a year all his money, property, attendants and horses were gone.

The old lady had begun to treat him coldly, but the girl seemed more devoted to him than ever. One day she said to him: "We have been together a year, but I am still not with child. They say that the spirit of the Bamboo Grove answers prayers as surely as an echo. Shall we go to his temple and offer a libation?"

Not suspecting any plot, the young man was delighted. And having pawned his coat to buy wine and sacrificial meat, he went with her to the temple and prayed to the spirit. They spent two nights there and started back the third day, the young man riding a donkey behind the girl's carriage. When they reached the north gate of the Hsuanyang quarter, she turned to him and said: "My aunt's house is in a lane to the east near here. Suppose we rest there for a little?"

He fell in with her wishes, and they had not gone more than a hundred paces when he saw a wide drive and their servant stopped the carriage, saying: "We have arrived." The young man got down and was met by a man-servant who came out to ask who they were. When told that it was Mistress Li, he went back and announced her. Presently a woman of about forty came out.

She greeted our hero and asked: "Has my niece arrived?" The girl alighted from the carriage and her aunt welcomed her, saying: "Why haven't you been here for so long?" They exchanged glances and laughed. Then the girl introduced him to her aunt, after which they all went into a side garden near the western gate. There was a pavilion set in a profusion of bamboos and trees amid quiet pools and summer-houses.

"Does this garden belong to your aunt?" the young man asked.

The girl laughed, but instead of answering she spoke of something else.

Delicious tea and cakes were served. But almost at once a man galloped up on a Fergana horse which was all in a lather. "The old lady has been taken very ill," he gasped. "She is beginning to be delirious. You had better hurry back."

"I am so worried," said the girl to her aunt. "Let me take the horse and ride on ahead. Then I will send it back, and you and my husband can come along later." The young man was anxious to go with her, but the aunt whispered to her maid to stop him at the gate.

"My sister must be dead by now," she said. "You and I ought to discuss the funeral together. What good can you do by running after her in an emergency like this?" So he stayed, to discuss the funeral and mourning rites.

It grew late, but still the horse had not come back. "I wonder what can have happened?" said the aunt. "You had better hurry over to see. I will come on later."

The young man set out. When he reached the house he found the gate firmly locked and sealed. Astounded, he questioned the neighbours. "Mistress Li only rented this house," they told him. "When her lease was up, the landlord took it back, and she moved away. She left two days ago." But when he asked her new address, they did not know it.

He thought of hurrying back to the Hsuanyang quarter to question the aunt, but it was already too late. So he pawned some of his clothes to procure himself supper and a bed. He was too angry to sleep, however, and did not close his eyes from dusk till dawn. Early in the morning he rode on his donkey to the aunt's house, but although he knocked on the door for the time it takes for a meal,

no one answered. At last his loud shouts brought a footman slowly to the door. The young man immediately
asked for the aunt.

"She doesn't live here," answered the footman.

"But she was here yesterday evening," the young man
protested. "Are you trying to fool me?" He enquired
whose house it was.

"This is the residence of His Excellency Master Tsui.
Yesterday somebody hired his courtyard to entertain a
cousin coming from a distance, but they were gone before
nightfall."

Bewildered and nearly distracted, the young man did
not know what to do. He went back to his old lodgings
in the Pucheng quarter. The landlord was sorry for him
and offered to feed him; but in his despair he could eat
nothing, and after three days he fell seriously ill. In
another fortnight he was so weak that the landlord feared
he could not live, and carried him to the undertakers.
As he lay there at the point of death, all the undertakers
in the market pitied him and nursed him, until he was
well enough to walk with a stick.

The undertakers then hired him by the day to hold up
the mourning curtains, and in this way he earned just
enough to support himself. In a few months he grew quite
strong again, but the mourners' chants always made him
regret that he could not change places with the dead, and
he would burst out sobbing and weeping, unable to restrain his tears. When he went home he would imitate
their chants. Being a man of intelligence, he very soon
mastered the art and became the most expert mourner
in the whole capital.

It happened that the undertakers in the East and West
Markets at this time were rivals. The undertakers in the
East Market turned out magnificent hearses and biers —
in this respect they were unrivalled — but the mourners
they provided were rather poor. Hearing of our hero's
skill, the chief undertaker offered him twenty thousand

cash for his services; and the experts of the East Market
secretly taught the young man all the fresh tunes they
knew, singing in harmony with him. This went on in
secret for several weeks. Then the two chief undertakers
agreed to give an exhibition in Tienmen Street to see
which was the better. The loser would forfeit 50,000
cash to cover the cost of the refreshments provided. An
agreement to this effect was drawn up and duly
witnessed.

Tens of thousands of people gathered to watch the
contest. The chief of the quarter got wind of the pro-
ceedings and told the chief of police. The chief of police
told the city magistrate. Very soon all the citizens of the
capital were hurrying to the spot and every house in the
city was empty.

The exhibition started at dawn. Coaches, hearses, and
all kinds of funeral trappings had been displayed for a
whole morning, but still the undertakers from the West
Market could establish no superiority, and their chief
was filled with shame. He built a platform in the south
corner of the square, and a man with a long beard came
forward, holding a hand-bell and attended by several
assistants. He wagged his beard, raised his eyebrows,
folded his arms and bowed. Then, mounting the platform,
he sang the *White Horse* dirge. Proud of his skill, he
looked to right and to left as if he knew himself unrivalled.   Shouts of approval were heard on every side, and
he was convinced that he must be the best dirge singer
of his time who could not possibly be surpassed.

Presently the chief undertaker of the East Market built
a platform in the north corner of the square, and a young
man in a black cap came forward, accompanied by five
or six assistants and carrying a bunch of hearse-plumes
in his hand. This was our hero.

He adjusted his clothes, looked slowly up and down,
then cleared his throat and began to sing with an air of
diffidence. He sang the dirge *Dew on the Garlic*, and

his voice rose so shrill and clear that its echoes shook
the forest trees. Before he had finished the first verse,
all who heard were sobbing and hiding their tears. They
started jeering at the chief undertaker of the West Market
until, overcome by shame, he stealthily put down the
money he had forfeited and fled, to the amazement of the
crowd.

Now the emperor had recently ordered the governors
of outlying provinces to confer with him at the capital
once a year. This was called the "Yearly Reckoning."
Thus our hero's father happened to be at the capital too,
and he and some of his colleagues, discarding their official
robes and insignia, had slipped out to watch the contest.
With them was an old servant, the husband of the young
man's foster-nurse. Recognizing our hero's accent and
gait, he wanted to accost him but dared not and wept.
Surprised, the Lord of Yingyang asked him why he was
crying.

"Sir," replied the servant, "the young man who is
singing reminds me of your lost son."

"My son was murdered by robbers because I gave him
too much money," said the Lord of Yingyang. "This
cannot be he." So saying, he began to weep too and went
back to his lodging.

The old servant then went again to ask some of the
undertakers: "Who was that singer? Where did he learn
such skill?" They told him it was the son of such a one,
and when he asked the young man's own name, that too
was unfamiliar. The old servant was so much puzzled
that he determined to put the matter to the test for himself. But when the young man saw him he gave a start,
and tried to hide in the crowd. The servant caught hold
of his sleeve, and said: "Surely it is you!" Then they
embraced and wept, and presently went back together.

But when the young man came to his father's lodging,
the Lord of Yingyang was angry with him and said:
"Your conduct has disgraced the family. How dare you

show your face again?" So saying he took him out of the
house and led him to the ground between Chuchiang and
Hsingyuan. Here he stripped him naked and gave him
several hundred strokes with his horse-whip, till the
young man succumbed to the pain and collapsed. Then
his father left, thinking he was dead.

However, the young man's singing-master had asked
some of his friends to keep a secret watch on him, and
now they came back and told the others what had happened. They were all greatly upset, and two men were
dispatched with a reed mat to bury him. When they got
there they found his heart still warm, and when they had
held him up for some time he started breathing again.
So they carried him home and gave him liquid food
through a reed pipe. The next morning he recovered
consciousness, but for a whole month he was unable to
move his hands and feet. Moreover, the sores left by his
thrashing festered and gave out such a stench that his
friends could not stand it, and one night they abandoned
him by the roadside.

The passers-by, however, took pity on him and threw
him scraps of food, so that he did not starve. After three
months he was well enough to hobble about with a stick.
Clad in a linen coat — which was knotted together in a
hundred places, so that it looked as tattered as a quail's
tail — and carrying a broken saucer in his hand, he
started to beg his way through the various quarters of
the city. Autumn had now turned to winter. He spent
his nights in lavatories and caves and his days haunting
the markets and booths.

One day when it was snowing hard, hunger and cold
had driven him into the streets. His bitter cry pierced all
who heard it to the heart. But the snow was so heavy
that hardly a house had its outer door open.

When he reached the eastern gate of the Anyi quarter,
he went north along the wall until he came to the seventh
or eighth house which he found had the left half of its

double door open. This was the house where the girl Li was then living, although the young man did not know it.

He stood at the door wailing persistently. And hunger and cold had made his cry so pitiful that you could scarcely bear to hear it.

The girl heard it from her room, and said to her maid: "That is my lover. I know his voice." She flew to the door and found him there, so emaciated and covered with sores that he seemed scarcely human.

"Can it be you?" she exclaimed, deeply moved. The young man simply nodded, too overcome by anger and excitement to speak.

She threw her arms round his neck, then wrapped him in her own embroidered jacket, led him to the western chamber and said in a choked voice: "It is all my fault that this has happened to you." And with these words she swooned.

The old woman came hurrying over in great alarm, crying: "What is it?" When the girl told her who had come, she immediately raised objections. "Send him packing!" she cried. "What did you bring him in here for?"

But the girl looked grave and protested: "No! This is the son of a noble house. Once he rode in grand carriages and wore fine clothes. But within a year of coming to our house he lost all he had. And then we got rid of him by a contemptible trick. We have ruined his career and made him despised by his fellow men. The love of father and son is implanted by Heaven; yet because of us his father hardened his heart and tried to kill him, then abandoned him so that he was reduced to this state.

"Everyone in the land knows that it was I who brought him to this. The court is full of his relatives. Once the authorities come to investigate this business, we shall be ruined. And since we have deceived Heaven and injured men, no spirits will take our part. Do we want to offend the gods and bring such misfortune on ourselves?

"I have lived as your daughter for twenty years, and my earnings amount to nearly a thousand pieces of gold. You are over sixty now, and I would like to give you enough to cover your expenses for another twenty years to buy my freedom, so that I can live somewhere else with this young man. We will not go far away. I shall see to it that we are near enough to pay our respects to you both morning and evening."

The old woman saw that the girl's mind was made up, so she gave her consent. When she had paid her ransom, the girl had several hundred pieces of gold left, and with them she hired a few rooms, five doors to the north. Here she gave the young man a bath, changed his clothes, fed him first with hot gruel, which was easy to digest, and later on with cheese and milk.

In a few weeks she was giving him all the choicest delicacies of land and sea. She clothed him, too, in the finest caps, shoes and stockings she could buy. In a few months he began to put on weight, and by the end of the year his health was as good as ever.

One day the girl said to him: "Now you are strong again and have got back your nerve. Try to think how much you remember of your old literary studies."

After a moment's thought he answered: "About a quarter."

Then she ordered her carriage to be got ready, and the young man followed her on horseback. When they reached the classical bookshop at the side-gate south of the Flag Tower, she made him choose all the books he wanted, to the tune of a hundred pieces of gold. With these packed in the carriage, she drove home. She now bade him set aside all other cares, to give his whole mind to his studies. Every evening he pored over his books, with the girl at his side, and would not sleep before midnight. If she saw that he was tired, she would advise him to write a poem or ode by way of relaxation.

In two years he had thoroughly mastered his subjects, having read all the books in the kingdom. "Now I can go in for the examinations," he said.

But she answered, "No, you had better revise thoroughly, to be ready for all contingencies."

After another year, she said, "Now you may go."

He passed the examination with high distinction at the first attempt, and his reputation spread through the Ministry of Ceremony. Even older men, when they read his compositions, felt the greatest respect for him and wanted to become his friends.

But the girl said: "Wait a little! Nowadays when a bachelor of arts has passed his examination, he thinks he deserves to become a high official and enjoy fame throughout the empire. But your shady past puts you at a disadvantage beside your fellow scholars. You must sharpen your weapons, to win a second victory. Then you can rival the best scholars."

Then the young man worked harder than ever, and his reputation grew. That year there was a special examination to select scholars of outstanding talent from all parts of the empire. The young man took the paper on criticism of the government and advice to the emperor, and came out top. He was appointed Army Inspector at Chengtu. Many high government officials were now his friends.

When he was about to take up his post, the girl said to him: "Now that you have regained your proper status, I no longer feel I have injured you. Let me go back and look after the old lady till she dies. You must marry a girl from some great family, who is fit to sacrifice to your ancestors. Don't injure yourself by an imprudent match. Take care of yourself! I must leave you."

The young man burst into tears and said: "If you leave me, I shall cut my throat."

But still she insisted that they must part.

He pleaded with her even more passionately, until she said: "Very well. I will go with you across the river as far as Chienmen. Then you must send me back."

To that he consented.

In a few weeks they reached Chienmen. Before they left a proclamation had been issued announcing that the young man's father, who had been Governor of Chang-chou, had been summoned to the capital and appointed Governor of Chengtu and Inspector of Chienmen. Twelve days later, the governor of Chengtu reached Chienmen, and the young man sent in his card to the posting-station where he was staying. The Lord of Yingyang could not believe that this was his son, yet the card bore the names of the young man's father and grandfather, with their ranks and titles. He was astounded. He sent for his son and, when he arrived, fell on his neck and wept bitterly.

"Now you are my son again," he said, and asked him to tell his story. When he had heard it, the Lord of Yingyang was amazed and enquired where the girl was.

"She came this far with me," answered the young man. "But now she is going back again."

"That won't do," said his father.

The next day he took his son in his carriage to Chengtu but kept the girl at Chienmen, finding suitable lodgings for her. The following day he ordered a go-between to arrange the wedding and prepare the six ceremonies to welcome the bride. Thus they were duly married. In the years that followed the girl proved herself a devoted wife and competent house-keeper, who was loved by all her relations.

Some years later both the young man's parents died, and he showed such filial piety in his mourning that a divine fungus appeared on the roof of his mourning-hut and the grain in that district grew three ears on each stalk. · The local authorities reported this to the emperor, and informed him too that several dozen white swallows had nested in the rafters of our hero's roof. The emperor was so impressed that he immediately raised the young man's rank.

When the three years of mourning were over, he was successively promoted to various important posts. Within ten years he was governor of several provinces, while his wife was given the title Lady of Chienkuo. They had four sons, all of whom became high officials, the least successful of them becoming Governor of Taiyuan. All four sons married into great families, so that all their relations were powerful and prosperous and their good fortune was unequalled.

How amazing that a singsong girl should have shown a degree of constancy rarely surpassed by the heroines of old! It really takes one's breath away.

My great-uncle was Governor of Chinchou, an official in the Ministry of Finance, and later Inspector of Roads and Waterways. The hero of this story was his predecessor in these three posts, so that my great-uncle knew all the details of his adventures. One day during the Chen Yuan period (785-805), Li Kung-tso of Lunghsi and I happened to be talking of wives who had distinguished themselves by their integrity, and I told him the story of the Lady of Chienkuo. He listened with rapt attention, and asked me to write it down. So I took up my brush, dipped it into the ink, and jotted down this rough outline of the tale to preserve it. It was written in the eighth month of the year Yi Hai (795).

WU-SHUANG THE PEERLESS

Hsueh Tiao

L IU Chen, a courtier during the Chien Chung period
(780-783), had a nephew called Wang Hsien-ke
whom he brought up in his own family because Wang's
father had died. Liu's daughter Wu-shuang (the peerless)
was a few years younger than Wang and the two children
played together; while Liu's wife was so fond of her
nephew that she gave him pet names. Several years
passed, during which Liu was as kind as could be to his
widowed sister and her son.

One day Wang's mother fell ill, and as she lay dying
she said to Liu: "I have only this one child, and you know
how I love him. I am sorry that I shan't live to see him
marry. Wu-shuang is a beautiful, intelligent girl, and
I love her dearly too. Don't marry her into any other
family. I entrust my son to you. If you consent to their
marriage, I shall die content."

"Set your mind at rest — you will recover," said Liu.
"Don't worry about anything else." But the lad's mother
died, and Wang took her coffin back to his house ·at
Hsiangyang for burial.

After the three years' mourning, he thought: "I am all
alone in the world. I had better take a wife and have
children. Wu-shuang is old enough to marry, and my
uncle surely won't go back on his word even though he
is now a high official." So he got his luggage ready and
went to the capital.

Hsueh Tiao (830-872), a native of Ho Chung (present-day
Shansi Province), was a scholar of the Imperial Academy.

By this time Liu was land tax commissioner and had a magnificent mansion, crowded with high-ranking visitors. When Wang called on him, Liu lodged him in the family school with his own children. But although acknowledged as his nephew, for a long time the young man heard nothing about the marriage. He had caught one glimpse of Wu-shuang from a window and she was as radiantly beautiful as a goddess come down to earth. He fell madly in love with her; but, afraid his uncle would not consent to their marriage, sold all that he had to raise several million cash. With this money he tipped his uncle's and aunt's attendants and servants lavishly, and gave feasts and drinking parties until he had gained free access to the inner court of the house. He also treated the cousins among whom he lived with the greatest respect. On his aunt's birthday, he pleased her by buying novel and rare presents — trinkets of carved rhinoceros horn and jade. And about ten days later, he sent an old woman to her to ask for Wu-shuang's hand.

"This is what I want too," said his aunt. "We must have a talk about it."

A few days later a servant informed him, "The mistress has been talking to the master about the marriage. But, judging by the way the master behaved, there seems to be some hitch." When Wang heard this he fell into despair and could not sleep all night, for fear his uncle would refuse him. However, he went on doing his best to please him.

One day Liu went to the court but came galloping home at dawn, perspiring and out of breath, able only to gasp: "Bolt the gate! Bolt the gate!" The whole household was thrown into confusion, and no one could guess what had happened. Presently Liu told them, "The troops at Chingyuan have revolted, and Yao Ling-yen has entered the Hanyuan Hall in the imperial court with an armed force! The emperor has left the palace by the North Gate, and all his ministers have fled with him. Concern for

my wife and daughter made me come back to put my
affairs in order. Call Hsien-ke at once to look after my
family, and I shall marry Wu-shuang to him."

At this Wang was surprised and overjoyed. He thanked
his uncle who, having loaded twenty baggage animals with
gold, silver and silk, said to him, "Change your clothes
and take these things out by Kaiyuan Gate, then hire
rooms in some quiet inn. I shall bring your aunt and
Wu-shuang after you by a roundabout route from Chihsia
Gate."

Wang did as he was told, waiting in an inn outside the
city; but by sunset they had still not arrived, and since
noonday the city gates had been closed. Tired of looking
south for the arrival of his uncle's family, Wang mounted
his horse and rode with a torch in his hand around the
city until he came to Chihsia Gate. This gate was bolted
too and there were guards there holding staffs, some
standing and some sitting.

"What has happened in the city?" he ventured to ask,
dismounting from his horse. "Has anyone passed this
way?"

"Marshal Chu Tse has made himself emperor," said one
guard. "In the afternoon a richly dressed man who had
four or five women with him tried to leave through this
gate. Everybody in the street knew him. They said he
was Liu, the land tax commissioner, so the officer in
charge dared not let him pass. Later in the evening
horsemen came to arrest him, and took all his family to
the north part of the city."

Wang burst out sobbing, and returned to his inn.
Towards midnight the city gates burst open and torches
shone bright as day as shouting soldiers armed with
swords and other weapons poured out to hunt down and
kill any runaway courtiers. Abandoning the baggage,
Wang fled in fright.

After three years spent in his country house at
Hsiangyang, when news came that the rebellion had been

suppressed, order restored in the capital and the whole empire pacified, he returned to Changan to find out what had become of his uncle. He had reached the south of the Hsinchang quarter and was reining in his horse, wondering where to go, when someone accosted him; and looking carefully he saw that it was his former servant Sai-hung. This Sai-hung had served Wang's father, and Liu finding him useful kept him on. Wang grasped his hand and they shed tears.

"Are my uncle and aunt well?" asked the young man.

"They are living in the Hsinhua quarter," Sai-hung told him.

Wang was overjoyed and cried, "I shall go there then."

"I am a freeman now," said Sai-hung. "I am staying with a man who has a small house of his own and make a living by selling silk. It is late. You had better spend the night with me, and we can go together tomorrow." Then Sai-hung took him to his house where they had a good meal with plenty to drink. Later in the evening word came that, because Liu had worked for the rebels, he and his wife had been executed while Wu-shuang had been taken to the palace as a maid.

In his grief Wang cried aloud till all the neighbours were moved to pity.

"Wide though the world is," he told Sai-hung, "I have no folk of my own. Where can I go?" Then he asked, "Are there any of the old family servants left?"

"Only Wu-shuang's maid Tsai-ping," replied Sai-hung. "She is working now in the house of General Wang, captain of the imperial guards."

"If I cannot see Wu-shuang again," sighed Wang, "I shall die content if only I can see her maid."

He paid a visit to the general, who had been his uncle's friend, told him the whole story from beginning to end and asked to redeem the maid with a good sum of money. The general was touched by his story, and agreed. Wang then rented a house, where he lived with Sai-hung and Tsai-ping.

One day Sai-hung said: "Young master, you are a grown man now, you should find some official post instead of moping at home all the time." Wang let himself be persuaded, and asked the general's help. The general recommended him to City Magistrate Li, and the latter was able to have him appointed magistrate of Fuping and concurrently master of the Changlo posting-station.

Several months later, a report came that a certain palace official was taking thirty handmaids to the mausoleum to set the place in good order. They would travel in ten curtained carriages and put up at the Changlo posting-station.

"I hear the palace maids selected are all girls from good families," Wang told Sai-hung. "I wonder if Wu-shuang is among them. Could you find out for me?"

"There are thousands of palace maids," retorted Sai-hung. "Why should Wu-shuang be one of these?"

"Go anyway," urged Wang. "You never know."

Sai-hung accordingly pretended to be a station officer and went to boil tea outside the curtain of the girls' room. Wang had given him three thousand cash and told him: "Stay by the stove. Don't leave the spot. And if you see her, report to me at once." But the palace maids kept out of sight on the other side of the curtain, and could only be heard talking together at night. When it grew late and all was still, Sai-hung washed his bowls and stoked his fire but dared not sleep. Suddenly someone called from the other side of the curtain: "Sai-hung! Sai-hung! How did you know I was here? Is my betrothed well?" Then there was the sound of sobbing.

"Our young master is now in charge of this posting-station," said Sai-hung. "He thought you might be here today, so he sent me with his greetings."

"I cannot say any more now," the girl replied. "Tomorrow after we leave, you will find a letter to my betrothed under the purple quilt in the northeast pavilion." After saying this she moved away. Presently he heard a great commotion inside and cries of "She has fainted!" The officer in charge shouted for a cordial. It was Wu-shuang who had fainted.

Sai-hung hurried to report this to Wang, who in desperation demanded, "How can I see her?"

"Wei Bridge is under repair," suggested Sai-hung. "You might pretend to be the officer in charge and stand near where the carriages pass. When Wu-shuang recognizes you, she will draw the curtain and you will see her."

Wang did as Sai-hung proposed. When the third carriage passed, the curtain was drawn and the sight of Wu-shuang filled him with grief and longing. Meantime Sai-hung had found the letter under the quilt in the pavilion. There were five sheets of paper with a printed design covered with the girl's writing and telling all that had befallen her and her utter misery. Wang shed bitter tears as he read it, certain in his heart that they would never meet again. But in a postscript to the letter she wrote, "I have heard that a bailiff named Ku in Fuping is a man you can turn to in trouble. Could you ask him to help?"

Wang requested his superior officer to relieve him of his duty at the posting-station, and went back to serve as magistrate of Fuping. He called on Bailiff Ku in his country house then for a whole year paid him frequent visits and tried in every way to please him, making him innumerable presents of embroidered silk and precious jewels. But not a word did he breathe all that time of his request. And when his term of office expired, he stayed on in the county.

One day Ku came to see him and said, "I'm a rough soldier, getting on in years. There's not much I can do for anyone. But you have treated me well, and I feel you must want something of me. I have a sense of chivalry, and I appreciate your friendship so much I mean to repay you even if it costs me my life."

Wang shed tears and bowed, then told him the whole story. When he had heard it, Ku looked up at the sky and clapped his head with his hand several times. "This is very difficult!" he exclaimed. "I shall try to help, but don't expect quick results."

Wang bowed again and responded, "If I can only see her again alive, I don't mind how long I have to wait."

Half a year passed without any news. Then one day there came a knock at Wang's door and a letter was delivered from Ku, which said, "My envoy to Mao Mountain has returned. Come over." Wang galloped there at once, but Ku said nothing. When asked about his envoy, he replied, "I have killed him. Drink some tea." Later that night he asked, "Do you have a maid in your house who knows Wu-shuang?" Wang told him that Tsai-ping did and at once had her brought there. After looking her over carefully, Ku smiled approvingly and said, "I shall borrow her for a few days. You may go back now."

A few days later it was rumoured that some high official had passed through the county, and one of the palace maids had been put to death. Filled with misgivings, Wang asked Sai-hung to make enquiries, and found that the girl executed was Wu-shuang. He wept and sobbed. "I had hoped that Ku could help," he sighed, "but now she is dead! What shall I do?" He shed tears and groaned, unable to restrain himself.

That same night, after midnight, Wang heard violent knocking at the door and when he opened it found Ku there with a stretcher.

"This is Wu-shuang," Ku told him. "To all appearances she is dead, but her heart is still warm. She will revive tomorrow, and you can give her some medicine. But you keep this quiet!" Wang carried the girl inside and kept watch. At dawn her limbs grew warm and she opened her eyes, but the sight of Wang made her cry out and faint away. He tended her and gave her cordials till night, when she recovered.

Ku told Wang, "Today I am repaying your kindness in full. I heard that a priest in Mao Mountain had a strange drug. Anyone who takes it appears to die suddenly but actually revives within three days. So I sent someone to ask for it, and managed to get one pill. Yesterday I asked Tsai-ping to disguise herself as an imperial envoy and give Wu-shuang this pill, ordering her to commit suicide because she was connected with the rebel party. At the mausoleum I pretended to be a relative, and redeemed her body with a hundred bolts of silk. I had to give big bribes to all the people on the way, to avoid being discovered. You must not stay here any longer. Outside the door you will find ten porters, five horses and two hundred bolts of silk. Take Wu-shuang away with you before dawn, changing your names and covering up your tracks to avoid trouble."

Before daybreak, Wang and Wu-shuang left. They travelled through the gorges until they reached Chiangling, where they stayed for some time. When they heard nothing from the capital to alarm them, Wang took his wife back to his country house at Hsiangyang, where they remained all their life and where they had many children.

There are many vicissitudes, strange encounters and separations in human life, but I have heard of nothing comparable to this story, which I often say is unique in history. Wu-shuang lost her freedom during troubled times, but Wang remained loyal to his love and finally won her, thanks to the strange measures taken by Ku. After overcoming so many difficulties, the young couple were eventually able to escape and return to their home, where they lived happily as husband and wife for fifty years. A remarkable story!

THE SPENDTHRIFT AND THE ALCHEMIST
Li Fu-yen

TU Tse-chun, who lived at the end of the Northern Chou Dynasty (557-581) and the beginning of the Sui Dynasty (581-617), was a young spendthrift who neglected his estate. Dissolute, fond of drinking and low pleasures, he soon squandered his fortune; and relatives whom he asked to take him in all turned him away because he refused to work. One winter day, ragged and hungry, he loitered till it was late at the west gate of the East Market, not knowing where to go. A picture of misery, he stood there looking up at the sky and sighing.

An old man with a stick came up and asked him, "Why are you sighing?"

Then Tu poured out his indignation at his relatives' heartlessness. His face revealed his feelings.

"How much money do you need?" asked the old man.

"I could manage with thirty or forty thousand," said Tu.

"That's not enough," said the old man. "Think again."

"A hundred thousand."

"That's not enough."

"A million."

"That's not enough."

"Three million."

"That's more like it," said the old man. He took some money from his sleeve and gave it to Tu, saying, "This is for tonight. Tomorrow at noon I shall wait for you at the

Li Fu-yen lived in the early part of the ninth century and wrote five books of tales and anecdotes.

Persian Hostel in the West Market. Be sure to come on time."

Tu went there punctually the next day, and sure enough the old man gave him three million cash, but then left without disclosing his name.

Now that he was rich, Tu became a spendthrift once more, confident that this vagabond life was over. He bought fine horses and rich clothes, and gathered boon companions to enjoy music and dancing in the courtesans' quarter. Not once did it occur to him to invest his money. In a couple of years he had nothing left and had to sell his rich clothes, carriages and horses to buy cheaper ones. Eventually he sold his last horse and bought a donkey, then sold his donkey to go on foot, until soon he was as destitute as ever.

Once again he did not know what to do, and could only lament his fate at the market gate. At once the old man appeared, grasped his hand and said, "What! Are you reduced to this again? Tell me how much you need, and I will help you."

Tu was ashamed to answer, and although the old man pressed him he kept declining. At last the old man said, "Come tomorrow at noon to where we met before."

Tu did so, in spite of his shame, and received ten million cash. Before accepting he was determined to turn over a new leaf and go into business so that he could outdo the richest men of old. But with money in his hands, he forgot his good resolutions and became as fond of pleasures as before. So in three or four years he was poorer than ever and once again met the old man in the same place. Overcome with shame, Tu hid his face and turned to go, but the old man took hold of his coat and stopped him, saying, "How badly you manage!" With that he gave him another thirty million, and said, "If this does not cure you, you must be beyond saving."

Tu thought, "I have led a dissolute life and run through all my property, and none of my relatives have ever helped me. Now here is this old man who has given me money three times — how can I repay him?" So he said to the old man, "With this sum I can settle my worldly affairs, make provision for my poor relatives and fulfil all my obligations. I am deeply grateful to you. After my affairs are settled, I shall do whatever you tell me."

"That is what I wish," was the old man's reply. "After you have settled your affairs, meet me on the fifteenth of the seventh month next year under the twin juniper trees in front of the Taoist temple."

As most of Tu's poor relatives lived in the southern Huai River valley, he bought more than one thousand five hundred acres of land near Yangchow, erected mansions in the suburbs of the city and built more than a hundred country villas by the chief highways. Having settled his poor relations there, he arranged marriages for his nephews and nieces and moved back to the ancestral burial place all members of the clan who had been buried outside. He repaid all who had helped him, too, and settled scores with old enemies. This done, he went to the temple on the date appointed.

He found the old man singing in the shade of the twin juniper trees, and together they set out for Yuntai Peak on Hua Mountain. After they had walked about fifteen miles they came to an imposing mansion which was obviously not the home of any common man. Bright clouds hovered over it and phoenixes and storks were flying there. In the central hall was a cauldron over nine feet high in which drugs were being brewed, and the purple flame cast a bright light on the windows. Around the cauldron stood magic figures of the Jade Virgins, the Green Dragons and the White Tigers.

It was now nearly sunset, and the old man took off his ordinary dress and revealed himself as a priest in a yellow cap and red cape. He gave Tu three white marble pills and a goblet of wine, then made him sit on a tiger skin by the west wall, facing east. "Be sure not to say a word!"

he warned him. "Not even if you see deities, devils, vampires, wild beasts, the horrors of hell, or your relatives bound and in agony — it will all be an illusion. But you must neither speak nor stir. Have no fear, for no harm will come to you. At all costs, remember what I have said." With that he disappeared. When Tu looked round the hall, he saw nothing but a huge jar filled with water.

The priest had no sooner gone than thousands of chariots and horsemen swept over the hills and valleys with flags flying and weapons gleaming. Their battle-cries shook heaven and earth. Their commander was over ten feet in height and both he and his charger were in gilded armour which dazzled the eye. This giant led several hundred warriors straight to the hall, where they unsheathed their swords and stretched taut their bows. "Who are you?" the commander roared at Tu. "How dare you confront me?" All the warriors rushed forward with drawn swords to demand Tu's name and reason for being there. But he said not a word. This so enraged them that furious yells of "Shoot him! Kill him!" resounded like thunder. Still he said not a word, and finally the commander withdrew, fuming with rage.

Then fierce tigers, deadly dragons, griffins, lions and tens of thousands of cobras rushed forward roaring and hissing, threatening to swallow Tu up or throw themselves on him. But not a muscle of his face moved, and soon these monsters vanished too.

Then torrential rain fell and the day grew dark. Lightning flashed around him and thunderbolts crashed beside him, until he could not open his eyes. The courtyard was presently more than ten feet deep in water which poured swift as lightning, loud as thunder, and irresistible as a deluge into the hall. In a flash the water had reached him. But Tu sat there ignoring it till the flood vanished too.

Then the commander returned, leading ox-headed jailers and other foul fiends from hell. They set a boiling cauldron before Tu and hemmed him in with long spears, swords and prongs. "If he will tell his name, let him go," ordered the commander. "Otherwise, run him through and throw him into the cauldron."

Still he said nothing.

Then they brought in his wife and threw her down at the foot of the steps leading to the hall. Pointing to her, they said to Tu, "Speak, and we will spare her."

Still he made no reply.

Then they whipped and beat her, shot and slashed her, burned and branded her, till her whole body was streaming with blood and she was in agony.

"I know I am only a simple woman and not good enough for you," she cried. "But I have served you for more than ten years. Now devils have seized me and the pain is more than I can bear. I would not ask you to lower yourself to plead with them; but if you say just one word, my life will be spared. How can you be so heartless and grudge even one word?" Tears poured down her cheeks as she reproached and cursed him. Still Tu paid no attention.

"Do you think I cannot kill her?" demanded the commander. Then he ordered the devils to fetch a chopper and chop off the woman's feet inch by inch. Tu's wife screamed with pain, but still he paid no attention.

"This scoundrel is well versed in magic," said the commander. "We cannot let him live." And he ordered his guards to kill Tu.

When Tu had been killed, his spirit was haled before the king of hell.

"Is this the wizard of Yuntai Peak?" asked the king of hell. "Put him to torture."

Then melted copper was poured down his throat, he was beaten with iron rods, pounded with pestles, ground between millstones, thrown into a fiery pit, boiled in a cauldron and dashed against a forest of swords. But through all his sufferings he bore in mind what the priest had said, and let no groan escape his lips. When the jailers announced that all the tortures had been tried, the king said, "This is a scoundrel. He must not be allowed to be a man. Let him be reborn as a woman in the family of Wang Ching, the magistrate of Shanfu County in Sungchou."

Then Tu was reborn as a woman. As a child she was delicate and often ill. Not for a single day was she free from painful medical treatment. Once she fell off the bed, and another time fell on to the stove. The pain was intense, but not a sound did she utter. She grew up into a beautiful girl but never spoke a word so that her family thought she had been born dumb. Her relatives insulted her in many ways, but she never retorted. A scholar from the same county, named Lu Kuei, heard of this dumb girl's beauty and sent a match-maker to ask for her hand. When the family declined because she was dumb, Lu said, "She doesn't have to speak to make a good wife. And she will be a good example for women who talk too much." Then the family agreed, and Lu married Tu with due ceremony. They came to love each other, and after they had been married several years Tu gave birth to a son. Soon the child was two years old, and amazingly precocious.

Lu could not believe that his wife was really dumb. One day, holding the child in his arms, he spoke to Tu, but the latter would not reply. Lu tried various ways to trick his wife into speaking, but still Tu remained silent. Then Lu flew into a rage and said, "In ancient times the Minister Chia had a wife who despised him and would never smile; but after seeing what a good hunter he was she changed her mind. Now I am not as bad as Chia, and my literary talents are much superior to skill in hunting; yet you refuse to speak to me. What use is a son, when the husband is despised by his wife?"

Thereupon, seizing the child's feet he dashed his head against a stone. The little boy's skull was smashed, and blood spurted out several feet. Love for the child made Tu forget the pledge and give an exclamation of horror.

While the exclamation was still on Tu's lips, he found himself back on the seat in the hall, with the priest before him. It was dawn. Purple flames from the cauldron were shooting up through the roof to the sky, and fire was rising from all sides to burn the house to ashes.

"Look what you have done! You have spoilt my work, you silly fellow!" exclaimed the priest. Seizing him by the hair, he threw Tu into a jar of water. Then the fire was extinguished.

"You succeeded in mastering joy, anger, sorrow, fear, hate and desire," said the priest. "Only love you could not overcome. If you had not cried out, my elixir would have been completed and you could have become immortal too. How hard it is to find a man who can attain godhead! Still I can brew my elixir again, while you remain a mortal and lead your own life on earth. Farewell!" Then he pointed out to Tu his way back.

Tu forced himself to look around. In the ruined cauldron was an iron rod as thick as a man's arm and several feet long. Taking off his outer garment, the priest began to cut this rod up with a knife.

After Tu's return to the world, he felt ashamed to have failed to repay the old man's kindness and swore to himself that he would make good his failure. But when he went back to Yuntai Peak there was no one there. He had to return sadly home.

THE KUN LUN SLAVE[1]

Pei Hsing

DURING the Ta Li period (766-779), there was a young
man called Tsui, a palace guard of the Thousand
Bulls Order, whose father was a high official and a close
friend of a minister. One day his father told him to call on
the minister to ask after his health. Now Tsui was a handsome young man, rather bashful and quiet but with a very
good manner. The minister ordered his maidservants to
raise the curtains and ask him in. And as Tsui bowed and
delivered his father's message, the minister took a fancy
to him; accordingly he made him sit down and talk.

There were three ravishingly beautiful maids there, who
peeled red peaches into golden bowls, then poured sweet-
ened cream over the peaches and presented them. The
minister ordered one maid who was dressed in red to take
a bowl to Tsui; but the young man was too shy in the
presence of girls to eat. Then the minister ordered the
girl in red to feed him with a spoon, and Tsui was forced
to eat a peach while the girl smiled teasingly.

When the youth rose to go, the minister said, "Come
again when you have time. Don't stand on ceremony." He
told the girl in red to see him out. Tsui looked back at
her as he left the courtyard, and she raised three fingers,
turned up the palm of one hand three times, then pointed

Pei Hsing lived during the second half of the ninth century.
He wrote or compiled three books of stories dealing mainly with
fairies and spirits.

[1] During the Tang Dynasty, slaves brought to China from the
South Seas were commonly known as Kun Lun slaves.

to the little mirror she wore on her breast and said,
"Remember!"

When Tsui had given his father an account of his visit,
he went back to his study lost in thought. He became
silent and low-spirited, and rapt in sad thoughts would
eat nothing. All he did was to chant a poem:

> Led by chance to a fairy mountain,
> I gazed into star-bright eyes.
> Through a red door the moon is shining,
> There forlorn a white beauty lies.

None of his servants knew what was on his mind.
But there was a Kun Lun slave in his family called Melek
who watched him for a time, then asked,

"What is troubling you that you look so sad all the
time? Why not tell your old slave?"

"What do fellows like you understand?" retorted Tsui.
"Why pry into my private affairs?"

"Just tell me," urged Melek, "and I promise to get you
what you want, be it far or near."

Impressed by his confident tone, Tsui told him the
whole story. "That's simple," said Melek. "Why didn't
you tell me earlier, instead of moping like that?"

When Tsui told him what signs the girl had made,
Melek said, "That's easy to understand. When she raised
three fingers, she meant that there are ten rooms in the
minister's house where the maids live, and she lives in
the third room. When she turned up one palm three times,
she was showing fifteen fingers, for the fifteenth of the
month. And the little mirror on her breast stood for the
full moon on the night of the fifteenth. That is when she
wants you to go to her."

Tsui was overjoyed. "Is there any way for me to satisfy
my longing?" he asked.

Melek smiled and said, "Tomorrow night is the
fifteenth. Give me two lengths of dark blue silk to make
two tightly fitting suits. The minister keeps a fierce dog

to guard the girls' quarters and kill any stranger who attempts to break in. It is one of the famous Haichou breed, swift as lightning and fierce as a tiger. I am the only man in the world who can kill this hound. Tonight I shall beat it to death for you."

Tsui gave him meat and wine and next evening he left, carrying an iron hammer with chains attached to it. After the time it takes for a meal he came back, saying, "The dog is dead. Now there is nothing to stop us."

Just before midnight, the slave helped Tsui to put on his dark blue suit, and with the young man on his back vaulted over about a dozen walls until they came to the girls' quarters. They stopped at the third room. The carved door was not locked, and the bronze lamp inside shed a faint light. They heard the girl sigh as she sat there expectantly. She was putting on emerald ear-rings and her face was newly rouged, but there was sadness in her face as she chanted:

Oh, the oriole cries as she longs for her love,
Who beneath the bright buds stole her jewel away;
Now the blue sky is cold and no message has come,
So she plays her jade flute every sorrowful day.

The guards were asleep and all was quiet. Tsui lifted the curtain and entered. For a moment the girl was speechless; then she jumped off the couch and grasping Tsui's hand said, "I knew a clever man like you would understand the signs I made with my fingers. But by what magic art did you come here?"

Tsui told her all the planning had been done by Melek, and that the Kun Lun slave had carried him there.

"Where is Melek?" asked the girl.

"Outside the curtain," he answered.

Then she asked Melek in, and offered him wine in a golden bowl.

"I come from the northern borderland and my family used to be rich," the girl told Tsui. "But my present

master was commander of the army there and forced me
to be his concubine. I am ashamed that I could not kill
myself and had to live on in disgrace. Though I powder
and rouge my face, my heart is always sad. We have fine
food in jade utensils and incense in golden censers; we
wear the softest silk and sleep under embroidered coverlets, and we have mother-of-pearl screens and jewels.
Yet these things cannot make me happy, when all the
time I feel I am a prisoner. Since your servant has this
strange skill, why not rescue me from my jail? If I were
free again, I could die content. But I would like to be
your slave, and have the honour of serving you. What do
you say, sir?"

Tsui changed colour and said nothing, but Melek
answered, "If your mind is made up, it is quite simple."

The girl was overjoyed.

Melek asked first to be allowed to take out her baggage. After he had made three trips, he said, "I fear it
will soon be dawn." Then with Tsui and the girl on his
back he vaulted over about a dozen high walls, just as
when they had come in. And all the time the minister's
guards heard nothing. Finally they returned to Tsui's
quarters, and hid the girl there.

The next morning, when the minister's household discovered that the girl was gone and the dog was dead, the
minister was appalled. "My house is always well guarded
and locked," he said, "yet now someone seems to have
flown in and out leaving no trace. This must be the work
of no common adventurer. Don't let word of this get out,
for fear harm should come of it."

The girl remained hidden in Tsui's house for two years.
Then, one spring day when she rode in a small carriage
to Chuchiang to see the flowers, she was recognized by
one of the minister's household. When the minister
learned of her whereabouts, he was amazed and summoned Tsui to question him. In fear and trembling, the
young man dared not conceal the truth, but told the

*The carved door was not locked, and the bronze
lamp inside shed a faint light*

minister the whole story and how he had been carried there by his slave.

"It was very wrong of the girl," said the minister. "But since she has served you so long, it is too late to demand justice. However I feel in duty bound to get rid of your Kun Lun slave: that man is a public menace."

Then he ordered fifty guards, armed to the teeth, to surround Tsui's house and capture the Kun Lun slave. But Melek, a dagger in his hand, vaulted over the wall as swiftly as if he had wings, like some huge bird of prey. Though arrows rained down, they all fell short, and in a flash he made good his escape.

Tsui's family was thrown into a panic. The minister too regretted what he had done, and was afraid. Every night for a whole year he had himself guarded by servants armed with swords and halberds.

Over ten years later, one of Tsui's household saw Melek selling medicine in the market at Loyang. He looked as vigorous as ever.

THE MAN WITH THE CURLY BEARD

Tu Kuang-ting

WHEN Emperor Yang of the Sui Dynasty (605-618) visited Yangchow, Councillor Yang Su was ordered to guard the West Capital. Now Yang Su, that proud noble, plumed himself on the fact that in those unsettled times no one in the empire had greater power or prestige than he. Giving free rein to his love of luxury and pride, he ceased to behave like a subject. He received both officials and guests seated on a couch, and went about supported by beautiful maids, in his behaviour usurping the emperor's prerogatives. He became worse, too, in his old age when, forgetting his duty to his sovereign, he made no attempt to save the realm from utter ruin.

One day Li Ching, later to become the Duke of Wei but then a private citizen, asked for an interview in order to offer advice on government policy. Yang Su, as usual, received him sitting. Li approached and said with a bow, "The empire is in a turmoil and the bold are contending for power. As chief councillor to the imperial house, Your Highness should be thinking of how to rally good men, and should not receive visitors sitting."

Yang Su was impressed and stood up to apologize. After talking with Li he was very pleased with him and accepted his memorandum.

Tu Kuang-ting (850-933) was a native of Chuchou (present-day Chekiang Province) who studied Taoism at Wutai Mountain in Shansi and later lived as a hermit in Chingcheng Mountain, Szechuan. Tu is reputed to have written many books, but only a few of his stories have come down to us.

Now while Li had been discoursing brilliantly, one of Yang's maids — a very beautiful girl who was standing in front of them holding a red whisk — had watched him intently. When he was leaving, she said to the officer at the door, "Ask him his name and where he lives." Li told the officer. The girl nodded and withdrew, and Li went back to his hostel.

That night, just before dawn, there was a soft knocking at Li's door, and when he got up he found a stranger there in a cap and a purple gown, who was carrying a stick and a bag. Asked who he was, the stranger said, "I am the maid with the red whisk in Councillor Yang's house." Then Li quickly let her in. When she took off her outer gown and cap, he saw she was a beautiful girl of about nineteen with a fair complexion, dressed in bright clothes. She bowed to him, and he returned the bow.

"I have served Yang Su for a long time," said the girl, "and seen many visitors. But there has never been any one like you. The vine cannot grow by itself, but needs a tree to cling to. So I have come to you."

"But Councillor Yang has great power in the capital; how can it be done?" said Li.

"Never mind him — he's an old imbecile," she replied. "Many maids have left, knowing that he will fall; and he makes very little effort to get them back. I have thought it over carefully. Don't you worry." Asked her name, she told Li it was Chang, and that she was the eldest in her family. He found her an angel in complexion, manner, speech and character. Both happy and alarmed at this unexpected conquest, he had not a moment's peace of mind. Inquisitive people kept peeping through his door, and for a few days a half-hearted search was made for her. Then Li and the girl dressed in fine clothes and fled on horseback from the capital to Taiyuan.

On the way they stopped at a hostel in Lingshih. The bed was made, meat was boiling in the pot, Chang was combing her long hair in front of the bed and Li was currying the horses at the door, when suddenly a man of medium height with a curly red beard rode up on a sorry-looking donkey. He threw down his leather bag before the fire, took a pillow and lay down on the bed to watch the girl comb her hair. Furious but uncertain what course to take, Li went on grooming the horses. The girl looked intently at the stranger's face, holding her hair in one hand while with the other she signed to Li behind her back to prevent his flaring up. Then, quickly pinning up her hair, she curtseyed to the stranger and asked his name. Still lying on the bed, he answered that it was Chang.

"My name is Chang too," she said. "We may be cousins." With a bow she asked his position in the family, and he told her he was the third child. When she informed him that she was the eldest in her family, the stranger laughed and replied, "Then you are the eldest of my younger cousins."

"Come and meet my cousin," she called to Li, who bowed to him and sat down with them by the fire.

"What are you boiling?" asked the stranger.

"Mutton. It should be cooked by now."

"I am famished," said the man with the curly beard. While Li went out to buy bread, he took a dagger from his waist and cut up the mutton. They ate together, and after they had finished the stranger sliced up what was left and gave it to the donkey. He was very quick in all his movements.

"You seem a poor fellow," the stranger remarked to Li. "How did you get hold of such a marvellous girl?"

"I may be poor but I am no fool," said Li. "I wouldn't tell anyone else, but I won't hide anything from you." And he described how it had come about.

"Where are you going now?" asked the other.

"To Taiyuan," said Li.

"By the way, I have come uninvited: have you any wine?"

Li told him that west of the hostel was a wineshop, and fetched him a pint of wine. As they ate together, he said to Li: "Judging by your looks and behaviour, you are a stout fellow. Do you know anybody remarkable in Taiyuan?"

"I used to know a man whom I thought truly great," replied Li. "My other friends are only fit to be generals and captains."

"What is his name?"

"His name is Li too."

"How old is he?"

"Only twenty."

"What is he now?"

"He is the son of a provincial general."

"He sounds like the man I am looking for," said the stranger. "But I will have to see him to make sure. Can you arrange a meeting?"

"I have a friend named Liu Wen-ching who knows him well," said Li. "We can arrange an interview through Liu. But why do you want to see him?"

"An astrologer told me there had been a strange portent at Taiyuan, and I should look into it. You are leaving tomorrow — when will you arrive?"

Li calculated how long it would take, and the stranger said, "Meet me at daybreak the day after you arrive at Fenyang Bridge." Then he got on his donkey and made off so swiftly that he was at once lost to sight.

Li and the girl were both amazed and delighted. "Such a brave fellow will not deceive us," they said. "We need not worry." After some time they whipped up their horses and left.

On the appointed day they entered the city of Taiyuan, and were very pleased to meet the stranger again. They went to find Liu, and told him, "A good fortune-teller wants to meet Li Shih-min.[1] Will you send for him?" Liu

---

[1] The founder of the Tang empire, who reigned from 627-649

thought highly of Li, so he immediately sent a messenger to him asking him to come. Presently Li Shih-min arrived, wearing neither coat nor shoes, but with a fur coat thrown over him. He was overflowing with good spirits, and his appearance was very striking.

The curly-bearded man, sitting silently at the end of the table, was struck from the moment of his entry. After drinking a few cups with him he called Li aside and said, "This is undoubtedly the future emperor." When Li told Liu this, the latter was overjoyed and highly pleased with himself too.

After Li Shih-min had left, the man with the curly beard declared, "I am eighty per cent certain, but my friend the Taoist priest must see him too. You two go back to the capital, but meet me one afternoon at the wineshop east of Mahang. If you see this donkey and another lean one, that means my priestly friend and I are there, and you can go straight up." Then he left, and again they did as they were told.

On the appointed day they went to the wineshop and saw the two donkeys. Lifting up the skirts of their robes they went upstairs, and found the curly-bearded man and a priest drinking there. They were pleased to see Li, asked him to sit down and drank about a dozen cups together.

"Downstairs in the cupboard," said the man with the curly beard, "you will find a hundred thousand cash. Get a quiet place to lodge your wife, and meet me again another day at Fenyang Bridge."

When Li went to the bridge, he found the priest and the curly-bearded man already there, and they went together to see Liu. They discovered him playing chess, and after greeting him they started chatting. Liu sent a note to invite Li Shih-min to watch the game. The priest played with Liu, while the curly-bearded man and Li watched.

When Li Shih-min arrived, his appearance struck awe into them all. He bowed and sat down, looking so serene

. . . his appearance struck awe into them all

and talking so well that the atmosphere seemed to freshen and splendour to be shed all around. At the sight of him the priest had turned pale, and as he made his next move he said, "It's all up with me. I have lost the game, and there's no help for it. What more is there to say?" He stopped playing and took his leave. Once outside he said to the curly-bearded man, "There is no place for you in this country. You had better try your luck elsewhere. Don't give up or lose hope." They decided to leave for the capital.

To Li the curly-bearded man said, "The day after you arrive, come with your wife to my humble lodgings. I know you have no property. I want to introduce my wife to you and talk things over. Be sure not to fail me." Then he sighed and left.

Li rode back to his lodgings. Later he went with his wife to the capital to call on the curly-bearded man. The latter's house had a small, plain wooden door. When they knocked, a man opened the door, bowed to them and said, "The master has been looking forward to your arrival for a long time." They were led through inner doors, each more magnificent than the last. Forty girl attendants stood in the court, and twenty slaves led the way to the east hall where they found a great display of rare and precious objects. There were so many fine caskets, cupboards, head-dresses, mirrors and trinkets that they felt they had left the world of men. After they had washed they changed into rich and strange garments, and then their host was announced. He came in wearing a gauze cap, with a fur coat thrown over him, his whole appearance magnificent and kingly. When they had greeted each other cordially, he called his wife to come out, and they discovered that she was a beauty too. They were invited into the central hall, where there was a fine feast spread — richer than the banquets given by princes — and while they feasted twenty women musicians played music which sounded as if made in paradise. When they had eaten their fill, wine was served. Then servants carried out from the ·east hall twenty couches covered with embroidered silk. They removed the covers, and Li saw that the couches were laden with account books and keys.

"This is all the treasure I possess," said the man with the curly beard. "I turn it all over to you. I meant to make my mark in the world, and fight with brave men for ten years or more to carve out a kingdom. But now that the true sovereign has been found, why should I stay here? Your friend Li Shih-min of Taiyuan will be a truly great ruler, who will restore peace to the empire after three or four years. With your outstanding gifts, if you do your best under his serene guidance, you will certainly reach the top rank of councillors. And your wife with her great beauty and discernment will win fame and honour through her illustrious husband. Only a woman like her could recognize your talent, and only a man like you could bring her glory. An able minister is bound to find a wise monarch. It is no accident that when the tiger roars the wind blows, and when the dragon bellows the clouds gather. You can use my gifts to help the true monarch and achieve great deeds. Go to it! Ten years from now, several hundred miles southeast of China, strange happenings will take place — that will be when I realize my ambition. When that time comes, will you both drink towards the southeast to congratulate me?" He bid his servants pay their respects to Li and his wife, saying, "From now on they are your master and mistress." Then the curly-bearded man and his wife put on military uniform and rode off, attended by one slave only. Soon they were out of sight.

Taking over the curly-bearded man's house, Li became wealthy and used his fortune to help Li Shih-min to conquer the whole empire.

During the Chen Kuan period (627-649), while Li was left minister and acting prime minister, the southern tribesmen reported that a thousand big ships and one

hundred thousand armed troops had entered the kingdom
of Fuyu, killed the king and occupied the land. By now all
was peaceful there again. Li realized that the curly-
bearded man had succeeded. On his return from court he
told his wife, and they put on ceremonial dress and drank
to the southeast to congratulate their old friend.

From this we see that imperial power is not won by
any great man who aspires to it, let alone any man who is
not great.   Any subject who vainly attempts to rebel is
like a praying mantis dashing itself against the wheel of
a chariot, for Heaven has willed that our empire should
prosper for a myriad generations.

It has been suggested that much of Li's military strat-
egy was taught him by the man with the curly beard.

Printed in the United States
1967